DANGER

DANGEROUS RIDE

SALLY DARROLL

Boxtree

First published in the UK 1990
by BOXTREE LIMITED, 36 Tavistock Street,
London WC2E 7PB

1 3 5 7 9 10 8 6 4 2

© William Collins Pty Ltd &
Amalgamated Television Services Pty 1989

Printed and bound in Great Britain by
The St Ives Group Plc

British Library Cataloguing in Publication Data
Darroll, Sally
Dangerous ride.
I. Title II. Series
813.914 [F]

ISBN 1–85283–074–3

1

It was a bright fine morning, with a bracing breeze coming in off the bay. Seagulls swooped and quarrelled on the beach, and pelicans fished near the jetty.

The seagulls and the pelicans could have been part of the scene in any one of a hundred Australian coastal towns, but, to its loyal residents, Summer Bay was something special.

To Summer Bay ears, even the seagulls had their own peculiar charm.

The seagulls weren't the only ones quarrelling this morning, however. The McPhees were at it again.

Neville McPhee and his wife Floss were always squabbling about something. Floss's open-handedness and robust sense of humour sometimes jarred Neville; just as Neville's performances on the bagpipes and his close-fisted attitude often jarred on Floss. So it wasn't surprising that hard words frequently echoed around their van at the Summer Bay Caravan Park.

No-one ever took them very seriously, and

especially not the Fletchers, who owned the park.

Tom and Pippa and their family had moved to the district quite recently, when Tom's retrenchment from his job in the city had suddenly threatened the existence of their much-loved foster family. Faced with losing the kids, Tom and Pippa had promptly moved to the country, to manage the rundown caravan park at Summer Bay.

In the months since they had arrived, they had made friends among the residents, and had become fond of many of their neighbours. Shortly after meeting the McPhees, Pippa had detected the underlying devotion of Neville to Floss. This was equalled only by the attachment of Floss to Neville, something Pippa understood very well.

So what if they chose to air their differences loudly and publicly? A working lifetime spent on the carnival circuit was hardly the place to breed partnerships of silence and discretion.

Floss might call a spade a spade, but she was as quick to help as she was to criticise, and Pippa was a great believer in talking things over.

So even if Pippa and Tom had heard this morning's argument, they would merely have shrugged and smiled indulgently. The McPhees were permanent residents at the park, and personal friends besides.

And with five foster children to care for — not to speak of preparations for her own long-awaited first baby — Pippa had plenty to do without worrying about Floss and Neville.

If she had been listening, she might have noticed that this morning's quarrel was different. The muffled words grew louder as the door of the McPhee van opened and Neville and Floss came out. Neville's normally neat grey hair was ruffled into a cockatoo crest of annoyance and his glasses seemed to be fairly shooting sparks of displeasure. In one hand he grasped a large suitcase.

'Just think, will you, Floss?' he protested with the air of one who has said this many times before. 'Once more. Just think what you're doing.'

Floss turned to him with exasperation on her strongly featured face. During her carnival years, Floss had made great use of palmistry and crystal ball, and even in retirement she retained something of the look of the gypsy she pretended to be. Today she had enlivened her grey dress with a bright yellow scarf knotted at the neck.

'I've thought. I've thought,' she said loudly.

'No you haven't,' protested Neville doggedly. 'Taking a job looking after your own grandson!'

'Change the record, Neville,' ordered Floss. 'If your son hadn't been so damned stubborn and stiff-necked all these years . . .'

'*My son*! My son, is he now?' Neville's voice cracked with outrage. 'I s'pose you had nothing to do with him, woman!'

'Cutting us off,' swept on Floss. 'Not even inviting us to his wedding . . . What sort of bloody son would do that? His own parents!' A tear sparkled in her eye and she dabbed it away.

3

'All right, all right,' muttered Neville. Floss was right. What kind of son *was* Scotty never to have contacted them in twenty years? Where had they gone wrong?

But all the same, Neville cursed the fates about what had happened the very day Floss had decided to force herself on Scotty's attention. She had conned Neville into visiting the city, and where had they ended up? On the doorstep of Scotty McPhee's mansion, that's where! Or at least Floss had.

Neville had remained determinedly in the car. Now he wished he had not. Scotty and his wife had been away, and the housekeeper who had answered the door had assumed Floss to be an applicant for the post of temporary nanny. And Floss, by some devious wheeling and dealing concerning Pippa Fletcher and Ailsa Hogan, had won the job.

Nanny to her own grandson! What would Scotty say when he found out?

'I'm the one who'll have to pick up the pieces,' muttered Neville.

'And I'm the one taking the risk,' snapped Floss. 'I'll pick myself up if I have to ... Hello, girls!'

Neville looked up at her change of tone as she greeted two of the Fletcher kids — Lynn and Carly. He smiled at them unwillingly. It wasn't *their* fault Floss was behaving like a chook with its head cut off.

'Hi. It's the big day, is it?' said Carly, the elder girl. She was sixteen, with fashionably shaggy hair falling over her shoulders and forehead. Large geometric earrings dangled among the hair and her normally rather sullen expression was replaced by one of lively interest.

'Yep!' agreed Floss proudly. She sounded highly confident, and Neville rolled his eyes and snorted disgustedly as he loaded the suitcase into the car.

'Are you sure they won't know who you are?' asked Lynn dubiously. She was thirteen, with a deceptively meek smooth-haired look. It always astonished Floss to remember that before she had come to live with the Fletchers, Lynn had been an unwanted runaway. Some trace of those desperate days still showed in occasional flashes of doubt and reserve.

But Floss was too full of her own adventure today to ponder about Lynn. 'Not a chance,' she scoffed. 'Our son's overseas, 'n' none of his friends have ever been allowed to see us.'

'I think that's terrible...' began Lynn indignantly.

'He sounds like a jerk to me,' said Carly roundly.

Floss shrugged. 'Well ... he thought he had his reasons,' she said vaguely. What they might have been she wouldn't consider. It hurt too much. 'Still,' she added hastily, 'things sometimes just work out right anyway... they're meant to be, you know. Like Scotty being away and me having a chance to meet Ben.'

'Did you see it in the cards?' asked Carly half-seriously.

'You don't need cards to see a flaming disaster,' chipped in Neville grumpily.

'I'm not changing my mind, Neville,' said Floss. 'So you might as well save your breath.'

Neville glared, but he knew when he was beaten, so he got into the car. 'You girls going somewhere?' he asked, glancing up at Carly and Lynn.

'Just to help out Mrs Pappas on the farm,' said Carly.

'Want a lift?' asked Neville. He was tired of arguing with Floss, and he hoped the company of the two girls would ease the atmosphere. He knew this ill-advised scheme was going to end in disaster.

'Sure, thanks,' said Carly. She and Lynn climbed into the back seat.

'How will you get back?' asked Floss.

Carly shrugged airily. 'I don't know... somehow,' she said confidently. 'We'll be right.'

Neville put the car in gear and pulled slowly out of the caravan park and into the street.

'Look, there's Frank!' called Lynn, pointing across the road. 'Just going into Ailsa's store.'

'Wish me luck, Frank!' yelled Floss.

The girls' dark, good-looking foster brother started, then grinned and waved. 'The best, Floss!' he called back.

Like the rest of the family, he wished Floss well and hoped Neville was wrong. If not, Floss was in for a very big disappointment.

As the McPhee car continued down the street, Frank's grin died away, and he pushed through the doorway of Hogan's General Store. He liked Ailsa Hogan, but it was difficult to forget that if it hadn't been for her Ruth Stewart might still have been in Summer Bay.

Of course, Roo had brought it on herself.

Frank had always known that Roo hated and resented the fact that Ailsa was her father's fiancée. In her view no-one was good enough to replace her dead mother. So, when she and her aunt Celia had discovered a shameful secret dating from Ailsa's girlhood, she had certainly had no compunction about using her knowledge to ruin Alf and Ailsa's engagement party.

What wounded Frank was the way Roo had lied, using and manipulating him to hurt Ailsa and her father.

So finally Roo had been exiled to boarding school. It was her own fault, and Frank knew he'd been played for a sucker.

Sighing deeply, he entered the shop. Ailsa smiled. 'How's it going, Frank?'

He shrugged, 'Okay.'

'What can I get for you?'

'Just a couple of things for Pippa,' replied Frank.

There was a small silence while he looked around the shelves. Then Ailsa cleared her throat. 'How's the band going?'

'Oh... gone off the boil since variety night,' said Frank ruefully. 'We had a couple of rehearsals this week, but it's all a bit dead.' He shrugged.

Until recently, Roo had been lead singer of the band.

'I thought you were really great,' said Ailsa warmly.

Frank rather agreed with her, but he didn't say so. He was only too aware that the band might have folded

7

completely when Roo left, if it hadn't been for Pippa. Whoever would have suspected his foster mother of having such a great voice? Her warm and friendly personality did the band no harm, either.

'What'll you do next?' enquired Ailsa.

'Dunno,' said Frank. 'Maybe some local gigs, if anyone wants us.'

'With Pippa?' asked Ailsa archly.

Frank shrugged. 'Lance and Martin are pushing for her to front the band full time. Pippa thinks it's a bit of a joke.'

Ailsa was surprised that Lance and Martin, the knockabout comedy duo of Summer Bay, should hold such a sensible opinion. 'What about you?' she asked.

'She could do it,' said Frank judiciously. 'She's got a great voice... I just don't know if anyone's keen enough to make it all work.'

Well, well! thought Ailsa. That didn't sound like Frank. His ambition had all seemed centred on one thing: to front a rock band.

'You're really full of cheer today, aren't you...?' she said. 'Nothing to do with a certain absent young person by any chance?'

Frank gave a shadow of his usual cheerful grin and shrugged.

'She's not in permanent exile, you know,' comforted Ailsa. 'Just boarding school. Everyone'll get over it. Including Alf.' She sighed as she spoke. Until her arrival, Alf had given all his love and attention to Roo. Too much, if results were anything to go by! She knew

8

he had been deeply hurt by his daughter's machinations.

Frank sounded unconvinced. 'Yeah... Still... I don't know, Ailsa. Can you start trusting someone again once you've stopped?'

'Depends how much you think they've changed,' said Ailsa sensibly. 'Oh...' her gaze wavered as Celia Stewart enterd. 'Hello, Celia.'

'Hello, Ailsa,' said Celia. She spoke rather more warmly than Ailsa had done. 'How are you, Frank? Will I guess? You were discussing Ruth?'

Frank turned away and picked up a couple of packets from the nearest shelf. 'I'll just have these, thanks,' he said, thrusting them at Ailsa.

Celia looked understanding and sympathetic, and moved closer, her high forehead under its pulled-back straight hair wrinkling with emotion. Frank flinched. He had no wish to be understood by Celia. She couldn't have been much older than Pippa, but it was difficult to believe that they belonged to the same species.

'Correct me if I'm wrong,' she was saying confidentially, 'but I had the impression you and Ruth were rather close.'

Frank glanced at the counter for inspiration. Talking to Ailsa was one thing. Being peeled by Celia was quite another. He noticed that Ailsa was glaring at Celia. Unfortunately, Celia's gaze was fixed on Frank.

'Three dollars twenty,' said Ailsa loudly.

Frank started, and handed over a five-dollar note.

As Ailsa turned away to get his change, Celia pounced. 'Remember, if you need someone to confide in...' She let her sentence trail off insinuatingly.

'Yeah. Right,' said Frank, reaching for his change.

'A sympathetic ear, an objective viewpoint...' continued Celia musingly.

'Thanks,' gulped Frank. He glanced helplessly at Ailsa. 'See you.' With another hunted glance at Celia, he turned and almost ran from the shop.

Her voice floated after him. 'I'm a good listener...'

Ailsa watched, between exasperation and amusement. She shook her head. 'That was a supersonic exit,' she said dryly. 'Well done.'

Celia bridled. 'I offered a compassionate ear. What's wrong with that?'

Ailsa's eyes rolled heavenward. She knew precisely why Frank had fled, but Celia would never understand, never in a million years.

2

Neville slowed down as they approached the driveway to the Pappas farm. 'Here be close enough?' he asked.

'Yeah, fine,' said Carly. 'Come on, Lynn. Oh, and thanks for the lift,' she added.

'You girls sure you'll be right, goin' home?' asked Floss, leaning out of the car window.

Carly hitched up her blue overalls. 'Yeah, 'course,' she said impatiently.

'Come on, woman. We can hardly offer them a lift home. We'll be in the city, remember,' said Neville edgily.

'You do take on, Nev,' said Floss. 'It's good of the kids to help Mrs Pappas out, seeing as her son can't do it any more.' She raised her voice. 'Too-roo then, girls! Be good!'

Lynn and Carly smiled weakly, then headed off up the driveway to the farm.

Ever since Nico Pappas had been taken to the mental home, they had been coming over to help his mother with the work around the farm. It made Lynn, at least, feel better to know that she was doing something for her friend.

Suddenly Carly, who was in front, stopped short. 'Well, look at that!' she exclaimed.

Lynn stared. A man in rough working clothes was carting a wheelbarrow-load of manure from the chook run. She blinked. Were her eyes okay? Could it really be Fisher? *Fisher*? Carting muck?

He certainly looked different from the sprucely autocratic deputy head *she* knew from school.

'Hello, Mr Fisher,' cooed Carly, grinning broadly. 'What are you doing?'

'Very much what it looks like, Miss Morris,' said Fisher dryly. 'Carting fowl manure. It's excellent for citrus trees, as you may or may not know.'

Carly rolled her eyes. That was old clever-clogs Fisher all right. Never could resist passing on information.

'You're helping Mrs Pappas too?' ventured Lynn.

'Is there any reason why I shouldn't?' asked Fisher smoothly.

'No...' said Lynn. Well, there wasn't. It just didn't seem very likely.

'It's hard for her to manage without Nico,' explained Fisher quietly.

Carly and Lynn glanced at one another. If Fisher hadn't got it into his head that Nico was the nut case who was poisoning animals at Summer Bay and whipped up public opinion on his side, Nico might not have been in hospital right now.

'I realise you regard me as partly responsible,' continued Fisher. 'It may interest you to hear me admit I feel partly responsible myself.'

Carly gawped. Fisher admitting to feeling responsible? Fisher admitting to guilt? *Fisher*? 'Well, um . . . well . . .' she muttered.

'Shut your mouth, Miss Morris. Fowl manure attracts flies,' said Fisher.

Carly gulped.

'Well.' Fisher changed his tone. Confession time was obviously over. 'Have you just come for the scenery or are you planning to help?'

'Oh . . . we'll help,' said Carly, coming to life.

'Might I suggest you begin by feeding the fowls?' said Fisher.

This was so clearly an order that Lynn scuttled off to the shed and filled a tin with wheat from the bin. When she returned, Carly was actually holding a post upright while Fisher swung the sledgehammer. Lynn winced as it smashed home on the butt end of the post, then scurried off to fetch a bucket of water.

She had no intention of working too closely with Fisher. She didn't trust his unusually amiable mood. It was almost as if the Hound of the Baskervilles had trotted up and asked to go 'walkies'!

It was some time later that she encountered Fisher again. His mild mood seemed to be persisting. 'I'm rather enjoying this,' he admitted.

'So am I,' managed Lynn.

'I wouldn't want to do it all the time,' Fisher added

hastily, 'but once in a while... it's rather pleasant. Come and help me with the fence.'

'All right,' said Lynn. She glanced at him apprehensively.

Fisher smiled rather grimly. 'Come, Miss Davenport. I'm not going to eat you,' he said.

'N-no, of course not,' said Lynn, but she didn't feel too sure!

Behind them, Carly watched in amazement. Lynn trotting off with Fisher? She didn't believe it. None of the kids at school would believe it either. No, impossible!

Carly shook her head and went back to work. Briefly, she wondered how Neville and Floss were faring. By now, they must have almost reached the posh suburb where their horrible son lived. How would the grandson — Ben — get along with Floss? Carly pulled a face.

She liked Floss — but as a grandma?

Unreal!

After Carly and Lynn got used to the idea of having Fisher as a work-mate instead of a slave-driver, the day at the Pappas farm passed quite agreeably. Trees were fertilised, fences mended, animals tended — all the many small jobs which had been neglected since Nico had been in the institution.

Poor Nico. He had never been brilliant, but he had been happy enough in his own way — until his beloved cow had met her death at the whim of a poisoner.

'We'd better go, I s'pose,' said Lynn, as the sun began to slant in the sky.

14

Carly nodded and pulled a face. Her back was stiff with bending. 'Okay.'

Water gushed from a tap behind them. Evidently Fisher had come to the same conclusion and was having a wash before he left for home.

Lynn tried to picture him doing normal things like sitting in front of the telly, eating meals — even having a bath. She snorted with amusement at the idea.

'See you tomorrow, sir,' called Carly with unusual politeness.

Fisher turned off the tap and looked up. 'If you wait five or ten minutes, I can give you a lift as far as the school.'

Carly flinched. She didn't fancy going anywhere with Fisher, not even the mild version they had worked with today. 'No, no, we'll be right thanks,' she said airily. 'We'll just hitch or something.'

Lynn glanced at her in surprise, but said nothing.

Fisher was not so reticent. Shaking the water from his hands, and still carrying his yellow-handled spade, he advanced on them. 'What did you say, young lady?' he demanded menacingly. The genial work-mate was gone. This was definitely the Fisher they knew and hated.

Carly pulled a face. She ought to've known.

'Don't you have any idea of the dangers involved in hitch-hiking?' asked Fisher harshly.

Carly gave an exaggerated sigh. 'If I don't he's about to tell me!' she muttered to Lynn.

'Apart from the normal risks, which are

considerable in any case,' went on Fisher, 'have you forgotten that someone with a distinctly twisted mind is at large in the district?'

Lynn looked indignantly at Carly. Of course they hadn't forgotten. Hadn't she just been thinking about poor Nico's cow? Hadn't that cow been poisoned by this very same nutter?

'No, we haven't forgotten,' began Carly, 'but...'

'Are your foster parents aware that you hitch-hike?' interrupted Fisher.

'Well, I haven't actually...'

Once again Fisher cut Carly off in mid-excuse. 'Stay there. Right there,' he ordered, pointing a bony finger at their feet. Lynn and Carly looked down automatically, then back at Fisher.

'Five more minutes,' he continued. 'You can afford that out of your busy schedule.' He glared at them both and then turned away.

'Yack, yack, yack,' mouthed Carly disgustedly, but there was no way out of it. They would have to travel with Fisher.

And travel with Fisher they did. Unfortunately, once started on a subject, Fisher could not let it alone. He continued to lecture them on the dangers of hitch-hiking all the way back to the school.

3

'There you are, young ladies,' said Fisher, pulling up just outside the school gates. 'I trust you can get yourselves home without further trouble?'

'Thanks,' said Lynn.

Carly just scowled. 'C'mon, let's go to Ailsa's,' she exploded when Fisher had closed the door. 'I've had it up to here.' She levelled her hand under her chin. 'Mr Tin Fart Fisher!'

She continued to moan all the way, and by the time they reached Hogan's store, Lynn was thoroughly sick of the subject. She hoped visiting Ailsa would take Carly's mind off it, but Carly wasn't giving up her grouch that easily. She followed Ailsa from counter to shelf to storeroom and back to the shelves again.

'And he went on all the way into school!' she raged as Ailsa began to take tins from a carton and stack them on the shelf.

Ailsa had evidently had enough too.

'Well he's right,' she said sensibly. 'You shouldn't hitch-hike. You know that.'

'But why say the same thing six hundred times!' complained Carly. 'It's not as if he cares about us. He's never wanted any of us here. You know that! He's been against us all, ever since we came . . .'

Ailsa sighed. She couldn't deny that Fisher had never been particularly welcoming to the Fletcher household.

'He certainly wouldn't want to see anything happen to you though,' she pointed out. 'Donald's a teacher through and through, and you're one of his students. In his book he *has* to care about you.'

Carly shook her head stubbornly. She wasn't about to give Fisher any credit at all. Lynn looked at her reproachfully. 'She's right, you know,' she said.

Traitor, thought Carly. Aloud, she tried another angle. 'He's got to be cracked,' she said. 'I mean, it's Saturday afternoon, and where does he go? Back to school to work!'

'There's probably a lot to do, with Wal Bertram away,' said Ailsa.

Lynn thought about the absent principal: so much more popular than Fisher. 'Do you think Mr Bertram'll ever come back?' she said wistfully.

'Who knows?' said Ailsa. 'He's near retiring age. He mightn't think it worth the trouble.'

'You never know where you are with Fisher,' complained Carly. 'One minute he's almost nice and the next he's a monster. He's nuts.'

'He's had a lot of unhappiness in his life,' said Ailsa. 'Don't forget. I went out with him for a while before I

18

got engaged to Alf. There's more to Donald Fisher than most people think.'

This caught the girls' interest, but Ailsa was clearly unsure about continuing.

'Go on,' urged Carly.

'It's personal,' said Ailsa shortly.

'Yeah, yeah,' said Carly. 'But you can't stop now.'

'How do you expect us to understand him,' if we don't know?' wheedled Lynn.

Ailsa laughed, remembering Frank's confrontation with Celia that morning.

Celia was not only a shover, she was an A-grade gossip. 'You'll have me as bad as Celia if you're not careful,' she said.

The girls stared at her, and Ailsa gave in. 'Okay. He was married at one stage, you know.'

Carly nodded. That wasn't news. 'One of Alf's sisters, wasn't it?' she said. 'Barbara.'

'What happened?' asked Lynn.

'Well, Barbara wanted to be a concert pianist,' said Ailsa. 'But marrying Donald killed that dream. She never settled down, so she finally left and took their daughter with her. Apparently he's been his lovable self ever since!'

'Funny, you never think of him with a family,' said Carly.

'Maybe he's starting to get better,' suggested Lynn. 'He was nice today. For a while, anyway. Do you know...' she broke off, but Ailsa looked enquiringly at her.

'At one time I thought he'd poisoned Nico's cow and our dog,' said Lynn. 'Mr Fisher, I mean.' She looked appealingly at Ailsa.

'No,' said Ailsa positively. 'Donald would never do that. It's not his way. I know it's hard for you two to take it in, but Donald Fisher's a decent man. In his way.'

'In his way?' snickered Carly.

'Well — I know now he didn't do it,' mumbled Lynn.

Ailsa nodded approvingly. 'No-one's all bad,' she said.

'We'd best be getting home,' said Lynn quickly. 'Come on, Carly.'

''Bye, girls,' said Ailsa.

The Fletcher household was as crowded and homely as ever. Lynn went up to the room she shared with Carly to change. As she tidied her plait, she mused over what Ailsa had said, and made a decision.

When she came down to the kitchen, Frank was sitting at the table poking at a small electrical gadget with a screwdriver. Carly was sprawled on the couch, reading a magazine. Lynn marched up to Carly.

'Well, I think I ought to tell him,' she said loudly.

'Hmm? What?' said Carly, startled.

'I think,' said Lynn determinedly, 'I ought to tell Mr Fisher I'm sorry I thought he poisoned our dog and Nico's cow.'

'Why, for heaven's sake?' asked Carly. So maybe old

Flathead had had a sad life. That didn't mean Lynn ought to go looking for trouble.

'You heard Ailsa,' said Lynn. 'Maybe he's not so bad.'

'Oh, for goodness sake!' exclaimed Carly. 'Fisher never even knew you thought that! Don't go telling him now!'

'He did,' persisted Lynn. 'I told him I did. So I should tell him I don't any more.'

Carly stared at her and then appealed to Frank. 'Can you deal with this? I'm busy!'

'I should tell him, shouldn't I Frank?' asked Lynn.

'Guess so,' said Frank.

'Don't say that!' said Carly.

'Nothing wrong with telling someone you made a mistake,' said Frank more firmly.

'There is when it's old Flathead,' said Carly.

Lynn raised her chin. 'Well, I'm going to find him now. Before I get cold feet,' she said firmly, and headed for the door.

'You're just after good marks,' scoffed Carly.

'Oh, let her do it if she wants to,' said Frank. 'Maybe it's a good sign.'

Carly looked blank. 'Of what?'

'Well...' Frank peered studiously at the interior of his gadget and shook it. 'You know the way she decided God was a bit of a dead loss for letting Nico cop it...'

'She's not the only one,' said Carly heavily.

'Yeah, but it doesn't bother you that much,' said

Frank. 'I mean it was important to her. God and all that. She's been going round thinking the world's a pretty lousy place.'

Carly thought about it. 'And you think she's starting to see it really isn't so bad after all?' she said.

'Let's hope so,' said Frank.

Fired up by what she was about to do, Lynn hurried back to the school. She wasn't quite sure what she expected to happen, but surely it would be something pretty good. In her mind she saw Fisher moved almost to the point of crying, patting her shoulder . . . Well no. Maybe not. Not Fisher. Lynn shook her head. But something like that.

As it happened, things turned out quite differently. Fisher was very startled to see her, and scarcely seemed to hear her stammered explanation. Lynn was quite bewildered, but Donald Fisher had other things on his mind.

He had just received a most disturbing phone call from the headmaster, Walter Bertram, who had recovered from his illness much more speedily than expected, and who actually intended to return to work.

Like Lynn, Fisher had been indulging in daydreams. Perhaps Walter wouldn't bother to return at all. And if he didn't — who better to take official control of Summer Bay High than the man who had stepped so capably into the breach some time before?

But now this dream was dissolving, and Fisher was

surprised at how hurt and bitter he felt. So at first he hardly noticed what Lynn Davenport was so earnestly trying to tell him.

'Well anyway I don't think it now,' stumbled Lynn.

Fisher paused. As Ailsa Hogan had pointed out, he was a teacher through and through. Sincerity and moral courage were to be encouraged in his students, so he put his disappointment behind him for the moment and looked down at Lynn.

'Thank you, Miss Davenport,' he said dryly. 'From among my many faults you can safely exclude poisoning animals. Now off you go.'

Lynn mumbled something and turned away. Fisher's hurt pride descended again like a grey blanket, and he left the building.

He didn't feel like working any more. What was the use? And talking of 'use', he could really 'use' a drink. Or two. Or even three.

Feeling depressed and unaccustomedly muzzy with alcohol, Fisher presently went down to the beach, where he sat staring moodily out to sea. He expected and wanted no company, but after a while a shadow fell over his clasped hands. He glanced up irritably to see Ailsa Hogan regarding him with some irony.

'Hello, Donald,' she said.

He grunted.

'Mind if I sit down?' asked Ailsa with elaborate courtesy.

Fisher made an effort. 'Be my guest,' he said. His usually crisp voice was faintly slurred.

Ailsa looked at him sideways. It seemed to be her day for hearing about other people's problems: Frank — upset about Ruth's exile; Carly — shooting her mouth off about Fisher; and now Fisher himself — sailing gloomily on an alcoholic sea.

'What's wrong?' she asked.

Fisher looked pained. 'Is it that obvious?' he asked.

'Not really,' lied Ailsa.

'But it's obvious to you,' said Fisher bitterly. 'Ailsa — everybody's mate. Always understands.'

'If you're in that sort of mood . . .' said Ailsa dryly.

Fisher changed his mind. 'No, stay — I need someone — been drowning my sorrows.'

Ailsa settled beside him on the sand, and he told her everything: the satisfaction he had found in his position as Acting Head, his fears that he had lost his chance and would always be passed over.

Ailsa listened patiently for a time. Then she said: 'I kind of wish you'd stop this, Donald. I don't think it's doing you any good.'

'Most other people get to wallow in self-pity now and again,' said Fisher. 'Why not me?'

She shrugged. 'Fair enough.'

'I'll quit,' said Fisher moodily.

'You'll what?'

'I'll threaten to quit.'

Ailsa put her arm round him comfortingly. 'Oh come on, don't be stupid,' she said.

'You're a good friend, Ailsa,' said Fisher in an alcoholic burst of gratitude.

Ailsa made a comical face to herself. At least none of the others had tried to use her as a pillow! Just as well no-one was around to see this display. Fisher would hate it.

Unfortunately, someone *was* around, and that someone was Alf Stewart's sister Celia, the biggest mouth in Summer Bay.

And Celia, having seen plenty but heard nothing, turned and raced back up the beach to her brother's liquor store.

'There's something I feel you ought to know, Alf,' she said ominously. 'About your fiancée. I've just seen her down on the beach with her arm around another man!'

Alf turned away from the shelves he was restocking, his face angry. 'Stop it, Celia,' he said flatly. 'Just stop right there. Enough is enough.'

'But Alf...'

'One of these days,' said Alf heavily, 'that tongue of yours is going to cause real trouble. You're going to hurt someone, real bad. You've got to put the lid on your need to blab about things that aren't your business.'

'I don't "blab",' said Celia indignantly. 'And I think it *is* my business when I see my brother's fiancée on the beach with another man!'

Alf sighed. He knew his Ailsa. 'Sis, can't you get it through your thick head — I don't care!'

'But what if she goes on like this when you're *married*?' wailed Celia.

'Look. Whatever Ailsa does, you can bet she's got a damned good reason for it.'

'As long as you're satisfied!' said Celia huffily.

'Celia,' said Alf through clenched teeth. 'I'm warning you!'

'I'll be on my way!' said Celia.

'That,' said Alf, 'is a very good idea. Goodbye.'

4

Lynn had returned from the school feeling very much better. She had cleared things up with Fisher, and so quietened the nagging of her conscience.

Lynn had a very active conscience: indeed, Carly often said it was much too lively for Lynn's own good! As she came into the caravan park, she noticed the McPhee car parked in its usual place. Neville must be home from the city.

Tomorrow, she planned, she'd go and visit Nico — maybe take him the present she had bought a few days before. Perhaps Carly would come with her.

The telephone shrilled as she entered the house. 'I'll get it!' called Lynn, and grabbed up the receiver.

'Hello — Lynn?' said a voice over the STD pips. 'Listen, love, it's Floss McPhee here. Could you possibly run out and tell Neville I'd like a word with him?'

'Just a moment,' said Lynn, and ran out to knock on the McPhee caravan door. Neville followed her into the kitchen. He was still annoyed, so he answered rather shortly.

Lynn went up to her bedroom, looking for Carly. She wanted to report her success with Fisher.

'Nev!' Floss's voice came loudly over the wires. Neville reflected that she barely needed to use the phone.

'How's it going?' he asked cautiously.

'He's a beaut little bloke, Nev: image of Scotty. The trouble is he just won't have a bar of me. If he knew who I was it'd be different, I'm sure.'

'You're not going to tell him!' exclaimed Neville.

'Of course not!' said Floss.

'Sounds like his father all right,' said Neville with irony.

'But you can't really blame him,' urged Floss. 'He doesn't know me from a bar of soap.'

'Look, why not just come home?' said Neville. 'Sounds like it's turning out the way I always said.'

There was a loud quacking sound of outrage, and Neville held the phone away from his ear.

'Everything'll be fine,' said Floss firmly, and hung up.

Neville put down the phone slowly, his face dark. Frank, who was still working at the table, looked up.

'Any problem?' he asked.

'No... Maybe... I dunno,' said Neville jerkily.

'How's Floss?' asked Frank.

'Oh... she's fine,' said Neville, but he didn't believe his own words.

•

28

Sunday at the Fletcher household meant a big Sunday roast and all the trimmings: part of Pippa Fletcher's intention to give her foster kids all the love and warmth and stability they had missed out on before. As she peeled the battalion of potatoes necessary to feed seven hungry people, she thought about the kids. They were good kids, really, whatever anyone said. And, despite their backgrounds, they were now her kids, hers and Tom's. A happy and stable present could go a long way to make up for an unhappy past. Tom himself was all the proof she needed of that.

Pippa's face softened, as it always did when she considered her husband. Abandoned at birth by his father and two years later by his mother, Tom could have turned out to be a real no-hoper. Instead, he had become the kind, sensitive man she loved, willing to take on five disturbed youngsters and treat them as his own.

The slap of sandalled feet made her look up as eight-year-old Sally tore into the kitchen in a flash of yellow skirts.

'Can you save those for me, please, Pippa?' she said breathlessly as she hurried through.

'Save what?' asked Pippa blankly, but Sally had gone. Her voice floated back. 'The potato peels...'

Pippa's lips framed a silent question: 'What on earth?', but she was used to Sally.

The next interruption came from Carly, who strolled in wearing her good skirt and jacket, with a black bow tied in her shaggy hair.

'Going somewhere?' asked Pippa, as Lynn followed, also dressed for visiting.

'Lynn wants to go and see Dummy . . .' began Carly.

'Nico,' corrected Lynn firmly.

Carly disregarded her. 'I thought I'd go too,' she said.

Pippa looked dubious. Ever since the poisoning business, Nico Pappas had been almost totally unresponsive. What was the use of visiting if he wasn't even aware of his surroundings?

Lynn rushed in to explain. 'The doctor said if we kept on coming, it might help him to sort of come back into the real world. I've got a present for him, too; it's out the back, so I'll just run and get it. Won't be a second.'

Lynn hurried out.

'I'm glad to see she's starting to do something instead of just sitting around and brooding about it,' said Pippa.

'Yeah,' said Carly. 'But what if Dummy . . .'

'Call him Nico,' corrected Pippa with a smile. Carly shrugged. Nico had always been several sandwiches short of a picnic, even before the present setback.

'What if he still doesn't know her?' Carly blurted. 'What if it makes no difference?'

'Then that's something she has to come to terms with,' said Pippa firmly. 'But if we're lucky, the doctor might be right, and he'll start to react to things.'

Carly picked up a potato. 'Yeah, well it must be really boring being a vegetable,' she said meaningfully.

Pippa also regarded the potatoes. 'Bad taste joke,' she reproved, but she smiled wryly.

Carly changed the subject. 'How often do buses come on Sundays?'

'Around here, every hour, on the hour,' returned Pippa.

Carly looked at her watch and exclaimed. 'It nearly *is* on the hour! Lynn! Hurry up!'

'Coming!' called Lynn. In a minute or two she arrived, carrying a painted cow in both hands.

'What's *that*?' asked Carly.

'It's a cow,' said Lynn innocently.

'I'm not blind,' scoffed Carly. 'I mean...'

'It's a present for Nico,' elaborated Lynn.

'I thought you said the nurses gave him a stuffed one or something?' said Carly.

'So? Now he'll have two,' said Lynn.

'He'll have a whole dairy farm by Christmas at this rate,' said Carly. 'Come on. We'll miss the bus.'

'Should I wrap it?' said Lynn doubtfully to Pippa.

Pippa glanced at her watch. Carly was hovering impatiently. 'Don't worry,' she said hastily. 'Just put it in the bag.'

'Come *on*, Lynn!' urged Carly.

Pippa dug in a cupboard and came out with a large plastic shopping bag. 'Here,' she said. 'Dum... Nico won't mind.'

'Let's *go*!' said Carly.

'Are you going to be back in time for lunch?' asked Pippa.

'Probably not,' said Carly over her shoulder. 'Sorry.'

'So long as you're here for dinner! Can't have the roast go to waste!' Pippa shook her head and began to count up potatoes, deciding thankfully that she'd already peeled enough. I'd better hurry, she thought, mentally going through the things she had to do.

Put lunch on, collect the laundry from the vans, go down and give a hand at the coffee shop which was part of Ailsa's store. Steven had gone there already. She hoped he was managing all right, although of course, in a family like theirs, everyone had to pull their weight.

Pippa picked up the vegetable board and tilted it to scrape the peelings into the bin.

'Hey, I want those, remember!' exclaimed Sally, coming back into the kitchen.

'Sorry,' said Pippa obediently, as Sally rescued the peelings. 'Er — we haven't acquired a pig, have we?' she asked with a broad grin.

'No, I want them for Lance,' said Sally.

'Lance wants potato peelings?' questioned Pippa, even more puzzled. Of course, only God and Lance knew why Lance did some of the things he did, but this was going too far.

'All he can get,' Sally was saying.

Pippa gave up. 'What for?'

'He likes them,' said Sally earnestly.

'But he bought twenty bags of potatoes the other day over at Ailsa's,' objected Pippa. 'I served him myself!'

Sally was losing interest. 'I guess he'll peel 'em, 'cos

he just wants the peels,' she said, clumsily wrapping the coveted peelings in the Sunday newspaper. Pippa just hoped Tom had finished reading it.

While Pippa and Sally debated the matter of the potato peelings, Carly and Lynn were hurrying down the driveway. Unfortunately for the girls, Martin and his faithful follower Lance were just coming up from the road. Martin, whose only claim to fame was that he was marginally brighter than Lance, made up for this with his enormous personal conceit. He smirked.

'G'day, Carls!' he said.

'Oh, no!' muttered Carly to Lynn, taking evasive action. Martin manoeuvred himself into her path, grinning fatuously. 'Come on, Carls, give us a break!' he drawled.

'Why?' said Carly.

'Didn't you like us at the variety night?' asked Lance, hurt.

'I didn't even *notice* you at the variety night,' said Carly crushingly.

'We were the hit!' said Lance.

'*Pippa* was the hit,' corrected Carly.

'She couldn't have done it without us but, eh?' boasted Martin.

'I liked you,' put in Lynn kindly.

'See?' said Martin to Carly.

She stepped around him.

'Listen, what's your problem?' asked Martin.

Carly gave him a shove. 'My only problem is I'm going to miss my bus because you're in my way.' She glared at Martin, grabbed Lynn by the elbow and hurried on.

Martin and Lance shrugged and went on towards their caravan, but by the time they had reached it they had managed to convince themselves that Carly was the one who had the problem, not them.

'Now we're even later,' fumed Carly, hurrying Lynn through the caravan park. 'That stupid Martin: really up himself!'

'Will we miss it?' asked Lynn, panting after her.

'Probably,' snapped Carly. As they reached the gate a station wagon belonging to one of the campers pulled up behind them. The driver stuck his head out.

'Where're you heading girls?'

'Down the coast,' said Carly hopefully.

'Want a lift?' asked the driver.

'Sure,' said Carly.

Lynn pulled at her sleeve. 'Do you think we should?' she hissed. 'You know what Mr Fisher said...'

Carly turned on her. 'Forget bloody Fisher! For heaven's sake, this guy's renting a caravan here!'

She walked round to the passenger door and opened it, smiling at the driver. 'Thanks,' she said gratefully.

'No problem,' he said.

Lynn frowned. What Carly said was quite right: the man had been staying there for days, but still... She shrugged and got in the back.

The car pulled away from the gate, past Ailsa's store and out of Summer Bay.

5

Sally ran happily out to the caravan where Lance lived, with the package of potato peelings under her arm. She met Lance and Martin at the doorway.

'I brought you some more,' she said triumphantly.

'Good on you, kid,' said Lance. He had a soft spot for Sally, who didn't take the mickey out of him like the other kids.

'Pippa nearly threw them away,' added Sally, climbing up the step. The whole van rocked as Lance and Martin joined her.

'Pippa?' said Lance foggily.

'Yeah, she just forgot,' said Sally.

'Forgot what?' asked Lance.

'Forgot you wanted them,' said Sally patiently.

'She knows?' said Lance uneasily. He knew that Pippa would certainly not approve of the use to which he was putting her potato peels. But all the same, a man had a right to a beer now and then, and if Alf Stewart cut off a man's supplies, what was a man to do? What this particular man had done was resurrect his granddad's old still. Wonderful homebrew you could make with a still. The only thing was — it needed about a thousand potato peelings!

'I told her to save them for you,' said Sally innocently. Lance gulped, but Sally continued: 'I'll bring you some more tomorrow. We always have potatoes. They must be cheap or something.'

'Thanks, kid,' said Lance uneasily.

Sally waved and went away.

'Listen, you'd better watch it,' said Martin.

'Yeah, yeah,' said Lance.

'If the kid shoots her mouth off too much, Tom'll get on to you,' warned Martin. 'You'll be out of here like a shot if he finds out you've got a still.'

Lance screwed up his face. 'What if I tell Pippa we've got a pig?' he said. 'Pigs like potato peels too.'

'Brilliant,' said Martin. 'Like, where?'

'Er — nah, you're right.' Lance shook his head, dismissing the idea. 'What if she asks though, eh? We better think of something to tell her...'

'We will, we will,' said Martin confidently. 'Just give me time, okay? Genius cannot be rushed, mate...'

Lance sighed contentedly. He had complete confidence in Martin.

Their ingenuity was tested quite soon. Lance's still was bubbling away merrily, digesting its offering of potato peelings. Lance adjusted a pipe or two and a spiral of bubbles resulted.

'Thought of anything yet, mate?' he asked.

'Nearly,' said Martin. He was staring out of the

window with a glazed expression. This altered suddenly to a look of horror. 'Hell! She's coming!' he exclaimed.

'Who?' said Lance.

'Pippa!'

'Ah gees . . .' Lance grabbed the curtain and pulled it across, screening the still from the caravan door. The still glooped gently.

'Turn it off!' hissed Martin.

Lance fiddled with taps and valves. 'I can't! I mean, it won't stop!' he said.

'All right, this is it, mate,' said Martin, taking command. 'Listen close. After considerin' all the alternatives. I reckon we've only got one option.'

'What, mate?' said Lance eagerly.

'Start eatin',' said Martin.

'You're jokin'?' said Lance.

Martin grabbed a plate and served a double handful of potato peelings onto it, topping it off with a generous squirt of sauce. 'Eat,' he ordered.

Lance looked at the unappetising plateful with distaste. '*You* eat,' he suggested.

Martin washed his hands of the situation. 'It's your rotten still,' he pointed out.

Lance wished it wasn't. He wavered, but a knock on the door sent him into frantic action. Pulling up his chair he began feverishly stuffing the peelings into his mouth.

'Can I come in?' called Pippa.

Martin opened the door.

'Thanks for these, Mrs F. They're yummy,' said Lance, chewing.

'You — ah — really like them?' said Pippa disbelievingly.

Lance nodded. 'Try some!' he offered.

'Thanks all the same,' said Pippa. The still gurgled behind the curtain. ''Scuse pigs,' said Lance desperately. 'These things give you wind.'

'Really good for you but,' chimed in Martin. 'All the vitamins are in the skin.'

Pippa gave up. The ways of Lance and Martin were beyond her. 'Well, I just came to get your sheets,' she said, moving to push aside the curtain. 'To wash.'

Lance choked, and leapt up to stop her. 'No — no. Leave 'em. I mean — I like dirty sheets. Comfortable. That's it.' He nodded emphatically. 'Comfortable.'

'Oh?' said Pippa. Light dawned. 'Oh, I see. Well, I wasn't born yesterday. You can give me the sheets later. When she leaves.'

'When who leaves?' asked Martin, looking puzzled.

Pippa jerked her thumb discreetly towards the curtained alcove. She dropped her voice. 'Lance's visitor.'

'Oh, yeah. Right,' said Martin, relieved that Pippa had furnished her own explanation. Though he did wonder what sort of visitor Pippa imagined to be making those weird blurping noises behind the curtain.

'I'm going over to help out at Ailsa's,' said Pippa loudly. 'Steven's there and maybe he could use a bit of a hand. Okay? Enjoy your — um — lunch!'

She grinned and left.

'That was close,' said Lance, shaken.

Martin leaned back and smiled smugly. 'Nah, under control all the way. I tell you, mate . . . it's genius that counts. Genius.'

Pippa hurried down the driveway and out along the road to Ailsa's store.

As she expected, Steven was busy with the cappuccino machine, which hummed and sloshed gently to itself like Lance's still. Steven, a curly-headed boy of around sixteen, looked up with some relief as his foster mother entered. Pippa wondered why. It wasn't as if the coffee shop was frantically busy. There was only one customer, young Sandra Barlow, who was in Steven's class at school. She was wearing a bright floral shirt, which combined with her golden red hair to make a cheerful note of colour. Not that Steven seemed to be deriving much pleasure from the sight!

'It's your sixth cappuccino,' he was saying severely. Pippa frowned at his rudeness.

'I like cappuccinos,' said Sandra.

Pippa smiled at her. 'Hello,' she said, and then went to join Steven. 'How's it going?'

'Pretty slow,' said Steven. 'No customers for ages.'

'What about her?' said Pippa, lowering her voice.

'Oh, that's just Sandra,' said Steven.

Pippa nodded intelligently. 'Ah.'

'This,' said Steven, 'is her sixth cappuccino.'

'I see,' said Pippa. 'Where's Ailsa?'

'Out the back,' said Steven moodily. 'Doing accounts or something.'

'I'll keep out of the way too, if you like,' offered Pippa.

'Don't you dare!' said Steven.

He carried the cup carefully over to Sandra's table, and then returned swiftly to Pippa. Sandra looked wistfully after him.

She looked like a pleasant girl, thought Pippa. She decided to give Steven a little push. 'Why don't you make yourself a coffee too?' she said in a low voice. 'Sit down and talk to her.'

'Why?' asked Steven, being difficult.

'Why not?' countered Pippa.

'What if we get a rush? What if a busload of people suddenly pours through the doors? Where would you be then?'

Pippa shrugged. She was disappointed in Steven. Sandra had sticking power though. She silently drank three more cappuccinos.

'Listen,' said Pippa. 'Why won't you just sit down and talk to her?'

'Because I don't really want to,' said Steven. His taste ran to older and more sophisticated girls. Unfortunately, they never reciprocated.

'Hasn't anyone ever told you to get lost?' asked Pippa.

Steven didn't answer. That was hitting below the belt.

'Remember how you felt?' persisted Pippa. 'You don't have to go overboard. Just be pleasant... And nine cappuccinos, that's got to be worth something.'

Silently, Steven made himself a cup of coffee. Silently, he walked over to Sandra's table. 'Mind if I sit down?' he asked.

Sandra raised a joyful face. ''Course not!' she said.

Away in the city, Floss McPhee was waiting just as patiently as Sandra for a boy to notice her. She had had one clash with Ben already: when he had ordered her to ask him before she made any phone calls. He had then played his computer game until she had sent him outside for some fresh air.

Left alone, Floss wandered restlessly about until her eye was caught by a red photo album on the shelf. The temptation was great. She took down the album and gazed hungrily at this record of Ben's childhood. She was still lost in the album, with tears in her eyes, when Ben came in abruptly.

'Why were you looking at that?' he asked in a hard voice.

Floss blew her nose. 'Give it back to me, Ben, and I'll put it back on the shelf,' she said steadily.

'It's ours,' said Ben furiously. 'What else have you been sticking your nose into?' He threw the album at her and ran outside.

Floss put it away carefully and then followed. 'Ben,' she said sternly.

41

'Leave me alone, you fat old bag,' said Ben clearly.

'Ben . . .'

'I hate you,' said Ben. 'Leave me alone.' He hit her on the arm.

Floss had had enough. She gave Ben one stinging slap on the leg. Unhesitatingly, he hit her back, then backed off and began to cry. 'I hate you,' he sobbed, and ran into the house, where he went straight to the telephone. After a few seconds of searching through the teledex, he began to punch buttons. There was a pause, and then his father's voice answered.

'Yes?' he said curtly. 'Who is it?'

'Dad, it's Ben,' he said quickly. He heard Floss enter the room and began to gabble: 'That woman . . . that Mrs Neville who's supposed to be taking care of me . . . she's really horrible, Dad, and she just hit me . . . She did! Yeah, you should see her! She's like an old witch . . . No, I'm serious.'

He didn't *look* serious: he was grinning as he held out the telephone to Floss. 'My father wants to speak to you,' he said.

She took the phone and, thinking quickly, began to speak in a Scottish accent. Firmly she explained that no, she wasn't accustomed to hitting children, and that Ben had been exceedingly rude.

It was quite painful to listen to her son's voice, after all this time, especially since he sounded so brusque and testy.

'Three o'clock in the morning, is it?' she said. 'No, I didn't know he was going to call you. Certainly.'

She handed the phone back to Ben.

'Hello, Dad?' said Ben expectantly. 'No, I know — but — Dad, listen.'

It was quite clear that Scotty McPhee was not listening. He was talking, and very angrily, too. Ben's expression changed to one of misery.

'Couldn't you come home, Daddy?' he said wistfully. 'Please come home.'

The phone barked again. Slowly Ben put it down, without saying goodbye. Then, hands clenched and shoulders stiff, he walked out of the room and sat down on the verandah steps.

After a moment or two Floss followed, and sat down beside him.

'They won't come home,' said Ben after a pause.

'You didn't want to spoil their holiday, did you?' said Floss soothingly.

Ben shrugged. They weren't doing much for his.

'So we're stuck with each other for a couple of weeks,' observed Floss. 'The way I see it, we can either fight it out the whole time. Or we can call a truce. What do you think?'

Ben shrugged again.

'How about a truce?' coaxed Floss.

Ben sighed. 'Okay,' he said.

'It doesn't mean you have to like me,' pointed out Floss sensibly. 'It just means we'll try and get along. That makes sense, doesn't it?'

Ben didn't answer, but Floss felt that at last she was making progress.

6

The man from the caravan park dropped Lynn and Carly a few hundred metres from the mental home where Nico Pappas was a patient. It was a fine old country house, which had been given over to the use of patients like Nico for some twenty years. Even so, it exuded quiet and peace.

Lynn looked up at it, hoping desperately that Nico was really going to benefit from the soothing atmosphere.

'Come on,' said Carly impatiently. 'Look! We've beaten the bus! Slow old thing.'

The bus on which they would have travelled had they not had a lift growled past the stop just outside the home.

There were no passengers waiting and apparently no-one wanted to get off, for it didn't stop, but lumbered on.

Lynn smoothed her hair with one hand and shook out her skirts. She had put on her nicest dress in Nico's honour. Clutching the bag containing the cow, she set off up the sweeping drive behind Carly.

When they came out again, some time later, Lynn was smiling and chattering happily to Carly. She was convinced that the visit had been a success.

'I got the feeling he knew us, Carly, didn't you? Just the way he looked at us . . . it was almost as if he was going to say something . . .'

'Well,' said Carly cautiously, 'the nurse said he was a bit better. She said it was a good thing you'd come to visit him.'

Lynn sighed happily. 'And the way he was holding the cow!' she continued. 'Stroking it, I mean. You could see he really liked it.'

'Yeah, he did,' said Carly. She was feeling just a little impatient with Lynn's enthusiasm, but suddenly she remembered what Frank had said the day before. 'See, things aren't all black, are they?' she pointed out.

Lynn didn't answer. Her hopeful smile wavered a little.

'Now look,' said Carly. 'Sometimes you've got to get on with things. Like coming here today. Don't you reckon you did Nico more good by coming to see him, bringing him that cow, than if you'd stayed at home moaning about how lousy it all is?'

'Ye-es,' said Lynn.

'*Well* then,' said Carly. 'Sometimes you've gotta take a risk. Take things into your own hands, that's all. Not just sit about waiting for everything to come to you.'

'The bus'll be coming to us soon,' ventured Lynn. 'P'r'aps we'd better hurry.'

46

'Oh hell yes!' They hurried down the drive to arrive panting at the bus stop. Carly looked at her watch and then at the timetable, then kicked the ground disgustedly. 'Ah, *hell*!' she said. 'We've just missed one. We've got to wait another hour now!'

'Oh well,' said Lynn. She sat down on the grass, clasping her skirt around her knees, making herself comfortable for the long wait.

Carly didn't join her, but prowled restlessly about the bus stop for a few moments, grumbling to herself and glaring at the timetable. Then suddenly she strode purposefully over to the side of the road and held up her thumb to a passing car.

'What're you *doing*?' gasped Lynn in alarm, as the car roared on by.

'Nyaah! Capitalist!' said Carly rudely, giving the retreating vehicle the two fingers. She held up her thumb again.

Lynn got up and tried to take her by the arm. 'Let's just wait, Carly,' she said anxiously. 'It doesn't matter.'

'Speak for yourself,' muttered Carly darkly. 'I don't want to sit around like a knot in a log if I don't have to.'

'But it's terribly dangerous to hitch-hike!' reminded Lynn. 'Mr Fisher said . . .'

Carly made a chopping motion with her hand.

'Not only him, Ailsa too — Pippa — 'continued Lynn.

Carly put her hands on her hips and gazed down at her. 'Listen,' she said patronisingly. 'I know what I'm doing, all right? There's two of us, don't forget? Everything'll be fine, you'll see!'

She stuck up her thumb again, just as a grey car passed by. It slowed down and drew up a little way ahead.

'Bingo!' said Carly jubilantly.

'Look, don't, all right?' said Lynn. She was seriously worried.

Carly turned on her. '*God*, you can be a goody-two-shoes!' she raged.

'Pippa'd go crazy if she knew,' said Lynn desperately.

'So she won't know,' said Carly. 'She'll think we caught the bus.' As she argued with Lynn, she kept glancing at the waiting car. What if the driver got fed up and drove away without them?

'Hurry up,' she nagged. 'We'll be here all day!'

'No,' said Lynn stubbornly, sitting down on the grass again.

'All right, *be* a pain then!' yelled Carly. She hurried off towards the grey car. The driver leaned across and opened the door, obviously inviting her to get in. Without looking back, Carly settled herself in the car.

The door shut with a final-sounding little clunk, and the car pulled away.

Miserably, Lynn gazed after it.

As the vehicle gathered speed, Carly made herself comfortable, before smiling sideways at the driver. He was quite young and good-looking: not much older than Frank. That was a bit of luck. She could have been picked up by some old guy who'd have lectured her all the way to Summer Bay.

'Going far?' he asked, glancing sideways at her.

Carly smiled. 'Nah, not all that,' she said. 'Summer Bay. Know it?'

The driver shrugged. 'Just passing through, chick,' he said.

'If you could just drop me off at the turnoff, that'll be great,' said Carly. 'Okay?'

'Whatever you say, chick,' he nodded.

'Fine,' said Carly. She leaned back comfortably, enjoying the play of the air conditioner on her face and hair. This was better than waiting for the flaming bus, she thought. She'd be home ages before Lynn. Briefly, she wondered how she'd explain that to Pippa, then shrugged. She only had to say that Lynn had decided to stay on with Dummy and catch a later bus, that was all. Lynn would back her up.

She crossed her legs and looked out the window. The driver didn't seem to want to talk much, which was fine with Carly. Occasionally the sea flashed into view between the trees at the side of the road. Carly hummed to herself.

She was thrown abruptly sideways as the car slowed and turned off the highway onto a narrow dirt road.

'Hey!' she said indignantly, as they bounced through ruts. The trees were thick. 'Where're you going?'

'Just a little short-cut I know, chick,' said the driver.

'Like hell!' said Carly. 'Get back on the road!'

'Sure,' said the driver, bringing the car to a sudden stop. 'Right away, chick. Just as soon's you 'n' me's had a little bit of fun. Call it a thank you for the nice ride, eh?'

49

'Like hell!' repeated Carly. She shoved the door open, but it crashed against a tree trunk, jamming her leg and losing her precious seconds. The man swore.

She was out and running for her life when she tripped over a protruding root. She fell heavily, crying out with pain as her chin hit the hard ground. Then she was scrabbling to her feet again, but it was too late. The driver of the car had her by the wrist and was forcing her down and laughing as he did so. He found her terror amusing.

That was the worst thing of all. He was laughing.

7

Sally was colouring in at the table when Lynn came home. It all seemed very quiet.

Lynn looked around. 'Where's Carly?' she asked.

'She went with you, didn't she?' said Sally, selecting a red marker.

Lynn stiffened. 'Yeah,' she said casually. 'But she didn't come back with me. She left earlier, so she should've got home ages ago.'

'Well, she hasn't come in yet,' said Sally.

Lynn wandered across the kitchen and looked out of the window. 'You sure?' she asked.

'Positive,' said Sally firmly. With an air of one who has better things to do than answer foolish questions, she returned to her colouring.

Lynn felt a cold clutch of apprehension in her insides. Carly had left the mental home an hour before she had, and, travelling by car, she should have been back long ago. 'Where are the others?' she asked.

Sally shrugged hugely. 'Pippa and Steven went back to Ailsa's after lunch,' she said. 'Frank and Tom are out in the yard somewhere. Bobby's in her van. She's coming here for tea, though.' She paused and sniffed. The heavy smell of roasting meat came from the kitchen. 'Smells yummy, doesn't it?'

'Oh . . . yeah,' said Lynn. She wondered if she ought to go out and find Bobby. Bobby had been closely involved with the Fletchers since their arrival at Summer Bay, and now she was part of the family. Her background was as bad as any of the other kids', but lately she seemed to have settled down.

Yes. Bobby would know what to do, reflected Lynn. But what if she was in one of her standoffish moods? You could never be sure, with Bobby.

When the door opened some time later, she turned round with anger and relief, but it was only Steven and Pippa, back from their afternoon stint at the coffee shop.

Pippa smiled at her. 'How was Nico?' she asked.

'Nico?' It all seemed so long ago to Lynn.

Pippa's smile broadened. 'Yes, Nico. You took him a cow, remember?'

'A little better,' said Lynn. And, as Pippa waited expectantly, she added, 'He liked the cow.'

'Sandra's okay you know, when you get talking to her,' said Steven casually.

To Lynn's relief, Pippa switched her attention to Steven. 'Thought you might say that,' she said with satisfaction.

'Did you know she's making a radio receiver in the science lab at school?' continued Steven.

'Who's Sandra?' asked Sally.

'No-one,' said Steven dismissively.

'A girl,' said Pippa. She rubbed her back and sat down in a chair with her legs stretched straight out. 'Where's Carly?' she asked.

'She'll ... um, she'll be back soon...' said Lynn. 'Nico really liked his cow.'

'So you said,' said Pippa. 'You're glad you went?'

'Yeah... it was great... fabulous!' said Lynn.

'Oh well, back to the drawing board,' said Pippa. 'The roast's about done, by the smell; better see to the trimmings.' She rose to her feet and went out to the kitchen.

Lynn went over to Steven. 'Listen,' she whispered, 'Carly hitched back. I'm worried.'

Sally, catching the urgency of her lowered tone, glanced up curiously. Steven shrugged. Carly wasn't his favourite person.

'She can look after herself,' he said.

'She should've been back ages ago,' persisted Lynn.

'Why didn't you tell Pippa?' queried Sally, wandering up to hang over the back of Steven's chair.

'She's probably just stopped off somewhere. Gone to see someone,' said Steven.

Sally looked solemn. 'Miss Patterson tells us never, ever, to get in a car with a stranger,' she said impressively.

'Yeah, right, Sal. You shouldn't,' said Lynn. She

53

turned back to Steven. 'Carly'll kill me if nothing's happened 'n' I've dobbed her in.'

'Don't panic yet,' advised Steven. 'Just leave it a bit longer.'

'But what if something really *has* happened?'

'Like what?' said Sally, round-eyed.

'Forget it, Sal,' said Steven. 'We'll give her till tea time. Okay?'

Lynn frowned.

'Okay?' repeated Steven impatiently.

Lynn nodded slowly. Yes, that was the best thing to do. But she still couldn't settle, and paced nervously back and forth while Sally continued to colour in and Steven lounged in his chair with a book.

'Would you eat potato peel?' asked Sally suddenly.

'If I was starving I guess I would,' said Steven.

'Lance is so funny,' said Sally confidentially. 'He says he'd eat potato peel any time.'

'If she's just stopped off somewhere, you'd think she'd have called up to say she'd be late,' said Lynn. 'I'll bet Pippa's going to ask me again and I'm going to have to say I don't know and...'

'Speak of the devil!' said Steven with emphasis. Lynn swung round. Carly had just come in.

'Carly! Where *were* you?' cried Lynn.

'Oh, sorry!' said Carly airily. 'I ran into Alison and she asked me over to her place for a while. Okay?'

'What did I tell you?' said Steven, going back to his book.

'You weren't worried, were you?' asked Carly.

54

'Of *course* I was worried!' said Lynn.

'Oh, Lynn — *really*!'

'Well, what was I supposed to think?' asked Lynn defensively.

Carly spun round. 'You didn't tell Pippa I'd hitched?'

'No.'

'Thanks,' said Carly sincerely. 'I'll just go and get cleaned up . . .' She went upstairs.

'There!' said Steven with satisfaction. 'Pays to keep your mouth shut sometimes.'

'Yeah,' said Lynn, but she wasn't convinced.

Lynn would have been even less happy if she could have seen Carly just then. Once safely in her bedroom, Carly had closed the door and allowed her carefully composed face to crumple.

For the first time in ages Carly — the tough one, the one who took things into her own hands and could look after herself — cried and cried.

Sunday dinner was an occasion for the Fletchers. When Tom came in, he went straight out to the kitchen to help Pippa. 'You kids can set the table,' he called back through the open door.

'That means you,' said Steven.

'Chauvinist,' accused Lynn.

'*I*,' said Steven loftily, 'have been working.'

'Chatting up Sandra,' translated Lynn. 'Here.' She shoved a handful of cutlery into his hand. 'Sal! Hey, Sal! Shift your drawing things!'

Sally grumbled, but began to gather up her markers, scrambling under the table for a dropped lid.

'And put them *away*,' insisted Lynn.

'After dinner,' bargained Sally.

'After dinner you're going to bed.'

Sally pulled a face and went away to her room.

Bobby and Frank came in. Steven put away his book and grudgingly laid the table. Tom stuck his head into the main room.

'Everyone here?' he asked, beaming, and pretended to count. 'Where're Sal and Carly?'

'Sal's putting her things away, and Carly's in our room,' said Lynn.

'Well, pop along and stir them up,' advised Tom. 'Pippa's dinner waits for no man and very few girls either.'

Lynn gave a small relieved grin. Just as well that question hadn't come half an hour before! She passed Sally on her way out and then turned the handle of the room she shared with Carly. It was locked. Lynn made a face. Carly was funny, sometimes. She rattled the handle. 'Come on, Carly! Tom says dinner's ready!'

There was a small silence. 'Coming!' called Carly. Lynn could hear her moving about. She gave the door another thump and went away.

•

After dinner, Tom, Bobby, Frank and Steven washed up while Pippa took Sally upstairs where she supervised her toothbrushing and saw her into bed. Of course Sally was quite capable of managing by herself, but Pippa could never forget that for many months poor Sally had had to manage for herself and her senile grandmother as well. Surely that entitled her to some extra spoiling now!

Tom looked up from his dishmop as Pippa came back down. 'Sal asleep?' he asked.

'Pretending to be,' smiled Pippa. 'Which is close enough.'

Tom let the water gurgle down the waste pipe and hung up his mop. 'Carly was quiet tonight,' he said thoughtfully. 'Hardly said boo all through dinner.'

'Mmm,' said Pippa, who hadn't really noticed. She moved across to lean against Tom and put her arm round him. 'Oh — you've finished,' she said.

Bobby shook back her rough dark hair and looked sardonic. 'Good timing,' she remarked. 'Don't suppose you want to do my homework for me to make up for it?'

Pippa grinned broadly. 'Not a chance!'

'Seem to waste all my time working these days,' grumbled Bobby. 'Whatever happened to night life?'

Frank grinned. 'Round here?' he asked sarcastically.

'Oh well, seeing as there's nothing else going, I'd better get on with it,' said Bobby. 'G'night.'

'Goodnight, Bob,' said Tom.

Bobby pulled an expressively downtrodden face and slouched out.

'How about you, Steven?' asked Tom. 'Done your homework?' He gave Pippa a hug. It was quite a while since the two of them had had some time to themselves. Maybe tonight?

'Ages ago,' said Steven.

'No revision or anything else to do?' asked Pippa hopefully.

'Nope!' said Steven. 'But I might go up and read for a bit, if you don't mind.'

'Good idea,' said Tom heartily. 'See you in the morning.'

'Goodnight,' said Steven.

'Well, that's the kids gone,' said Frank. 'Feel like a game of cards?'

'Ah ... no thanks, mate,' said Tom. 'I'm not really in the mood.'

'I'm easy,' said Frank, shrugging. 'What are you in the mood for?'

Tom and Pippa exchanged glances, and Pippa giggled.

'Oh,' said Frank, understanding. 'Right. Don't worry about me then... I'll just, er...' Searching for inspiration, he glanced at his watch. 'Gees, is that the time?' he said in well-simulated amazement. 'Nine o'clock already! And I've gotta work tomorrow.' He made his way out, but couldn't resist a parting dig. 'Speaking of work, you'd better not stay up too late yourself, Tom!'

Tom glared at him and clenched a menacing fist.

Frank flung up his hands in mock surrender. 'I'm going! I'm going!'

Tom and Pippa looked around the silent room with satisfaction. 'Peace at last!' said Tom.

But not for long. The door opened noisily and Bobby came in, carrying some school books. ''Scuse me, folks!' she said. 'Don't have any crib notes. Have to borrow Carly's.' She flipped a hand at Pippa and Tom, and bounced up the stairs. Pippa giggled. 'You were saying?' she said.

8

Bobby hurried up the stairs. She knew she ought to have done her homework on Friday night, but here she was again — nine o'clock Sunday night, with an essay to write. If it wasn't done, Fisher would give her curry in the morning.

Not that Bobby was afraid of Fisher: they were long-standing enemies, but she was no longer quite so fond of stirring up trouble.

She opened the door into Lynn and Carly's bedroom and, dumping her books, settled herself on the bed. Ostentatiously she took out a roneoed question sheet. She cleared her throat loudly and began to read: ' "As a treatise on ambition and power, Shakespeare's *Macbeth* is as relevant today as it was in 1606. Discuss." You got those crib notes, Carly?'

Carly shook her head.

'Well then, do you mind talkin' about it for a minute ... Fisher wants four hundred words on this. So far I've got one. "Yes." Great, huh?'

'Go away, Bobby,' said Carly wearily.

'Don't be a slag,' said Bobby angrily. 'You've got this essay too — what're *you* goin' to say?'

'Will you just buzz off!' snapped Carly.

'Well!' Bobby bounced off the bed and gathered up her books. 'Thanks for nothin'!'

She stormed through the door which had just been opened by Lynn, sleek and clean from her shower.

'What's wrong?' asked Lynn, concerned.

Carly stretched and got up. 'Have you finished with the bathroom?' she asked.

'Yes, sure,' said Lynn. 'But Carly — is anything wrong?'

Carly took her dressing gown off the peg behind the door and wandered out as if she hadn't heard.

Bobby thudded down the stairs three at a time. 'God, she can be a jerk sometimes!' she exclaimed, bursting into the main room.

Tom moved away from Pippa and rolled his eyes.

'Now I'm going to have to sit down and really *write* the bloody thing!' continued Bobby. She slumped down at the table and began to spread out her books.

'"As a treatise on ambition and power,"' she read in a bored voice, '"Shakespeare's *Macbeth* is as relevant today as it was in 1606." I guess I could just repeat the question, eh? That's at least eighteen words straight off. If you count "1606" as a word. Hey, Pippa, would you count that as a word?'

'You could write it out,' suggested Pippa. 'Sixteen hundred and six. It's four words then.'

'Hey! Good thinkin', top cat!' said Bobby admiringly. '"As a treatise on ambition and power..."'

Pippa raised her eyebrows at Tom and pantomimed despair. Tom just closed his eyes.

Carly seemed to be taking a long time in the shower, thought Lynn, as she got into bed and clasped her hands round her humped knees. She rested her chin on her hands and sighed, looking up sharply as Carly came in, wearing her dressing gown and still slightly damp around the edges.

'I thought you'd be asleep by now,' said Carly offhandedly.

'I'm not tired,' said Lynn. 'Hey, Carly...'

'Yes?' said Carly.

'How come you were so late home?'

'I told you. I went to see Alison. Just forgot how late it was. You know how it is, when you get talking?'

Lynn nodded. 'Are you sure?' she asked.

'Yes, Lynn,' said Carly. 'I'm sure.' She turned away from Lynn and began to get her uniform ready for school the next morning. Then she took off her dressing gown and hung it up, turned back the bedclothes and got into bed.

'You'd tell me, wouldn't you?' pleaded Lynn. 'If something was wrong?'

Carly smiled reassuringly. 'Of course I would,' she lied. 'Don't worry. Everything's fine.' She switched off

63

the light and got into bed, turning her back and effectively ending the conversation.

Lynn gave up and settled down with a sigh. She was soon asleep, but Carly lay staring into the darkness, reliving the moments of horror.

Carly slept very little, and in the morning she looked pale and edgy. Another shower made her feel a little better, but breakfast time seemed to last forever. When at last she escaped, her face felt stiff and strange from the effort of smiling. She kept well away from the rest of the family on the way to school, but Bobby caught up with her in the corridor.

'Wait up, Carly, what's your bloody hurry?' she grumbled.

Matt, one of the other students, whistled appreciatively. 'Hey, I like that ribbon you've got in your hair, Carls!'

Carly quickened her step, anxious to get away from them and their chatter.

'Hey, it's a compliment!' persisted Matt. 'Make the most of it, girl!' He reached out and tweaked the ribbon. Carly jumped and pulled away.

'Keep your hands to yourself,' she snarled and hurried off.

'What's up with her?' asked Matt blankly, looking at Bobby. 'What am I supposed to have done?'

Bobby shrugged, still sore at Carly's attitude the night before. 'Who knows?' she said. 'Sometimes I think she's a ravin' nutter. She's got a brain like a retarded goat sometimes!'

That day was always something of a blur to Carly. Despite all her efforts to act normally, she found herself constantly jumping and flinching whenever anyone spoke to her. She said very little to anyone.

At the house, Pippa made the most of the family's absence to clear up after the weekend. After lunch, she went around to give Ailsa a hand at the store. She looked up and smiled as Tom came in.

'Couple of loaves of bread and three litres of milk please, Miss,' said Tom solemnly.

'Right you are, sir,' said Pippa, 'anything you say sir, will that be all sir?'

'It'd better be,' said Tom, dropping the act. 'Those kids eat like starving dingoes!'

'That should last us until tomorrow, anyway,' said Pippa.

'What, with that mob? We should be so lucky!'

'Have you got time for a cup of coffee?' asked Pippa. 'Make you feel better.'

'Love to,' said Tom, 'but I can't. I've got to refill the gas bottles for the caravans. Can't have the guests running out of steam!'

'Dear me no!' Pippa sighed. 'One of these days, Tom, you and I are going to sit down and have a normal conversation that doesn't revolve entirely around work or the kids. If we haven't forgotten how.'

65

'You reckon?' said Tom.

'I reckon,' said Pippa firmly. 'Although I must admit that by the time *that* happens, I'll be toothless and you'll be bald.' She reached out and ruffled Tom's hair.

'It's getting to you, huh?' he said sympathetically, detecting the seriousness behind her light tone.

'Oh ... just a bit,' said Pippa. 'You know what I've been doing all day? Besides housework and serving at the shop I mean?'

'What?'

'I've been spending the whole time having daydreams about you and me in a decadently expensive restaurant having a romantic dinner for two. With positively no interruptions. Crazy, huh?'

'When do we book?' asked Tom.

'Never,' said Pippa gloomily. 'Oh go on, you fix the gas bottles. I promise I'll be in a better mood when I get home.'

'Done!' said Tom. 'I'll just drop this stuff off at the house and then get down to it.'

He gathered up the loaves of bread and cartons of milk in both arms and went out to find Frank. He had an idea.

Steven was the first to get home from school, and he settled down at the table to work on his maths homework. He wasn't left undisturbed for long — a few minutes later Lance and Martin arrived.

'Hey, Lance, want any more potato peels?' said Steven absently.

Lance jumped, 'Wh-what? Potato peels? What'd I be wantin' those for, mate?'

'To eat,' reminded Martin.

'Yeah, right, mate. That's it, I wanted 'em to eat,' said Lance. He looked puzzled. 'Was you sayin' somethin', Stevo?'

Steven groaned and rolled his eyes. 'Forget it, just forget it, Lance. Can you get off that book?' he added politely as Lance heaved himself up onto the table. 'I need it.'

Bobby came in just as Lance got off. 'Hi, guys,' she said. 'Helping Steve with his maths are you, Lance?'

'Where's Carly?' said Martin.

Bobby bristled. 'What's it to you?' she asked truculently as Carly came in slowly and headed for the stairs.

'Hey, Carls — what's the rush?' demanded Martin. 'Where're you going?'

Carly looked at him with distaste. 'Up to my room,' she said.

Martin swaggered over, ignoring Lynn, who was following Carly. 'Why go up there when the action's right down here?' said Martin fatuously. 'Let's quit playing games, Carly, baby . . . I can feel the vibes.' He smirked and thumped himself on the chest. 'I know you want me, Carls . . . let's just go for it!'

Masterfully, he grabbed her round the waist and bent her backwards in a Hollywood-style kiss. Lance watched enviously. He wished he had style like Martin!

The others accepted it as a bit of fun: just about par for the course with Martin, but for Carly it was like some clumsy echo of what had happened the day before.

'No! Let me go! Let go of me!' she shrieked, struggling. Her school bag hit the floor, a waterfall of books slithering out. Disconcerted, Martin let her go and stepped away with his hands held up, palms out.

'Hey, okay ... only jokin'!' he said.

Carly gave him a violent push that sent him cannoning into Lance and tore off up the stairs, sobbing loudly.

'Carly ...' said Lynn. She looked around helplessly at the others and then headed for the stairs. Bobby and Steven followed. They reached the girls' bedroom just in time to see Carly throw herself on the bed in a storm of tears. She couldn't pretend any longer.

Lynn sat down and patted Carly awkwardly on the shoulder.

'Hey — what's up? Carly? What's wrong?' said Steven.

Bobby turned on him fiercely. 'Get downstairs and deal with those two oafs ... get rid of 'em!' she hissed.

'What'll I tell them?' asked Steven.

'Hell, I dunno!' said Bobby. 'Tell 'em what you like. No — tell 'em she was pulling their legs — joke, see? Tell 'em everything's okay, but just get rid of 'em!'

With another worried look at Carly's heaving shoulders, Steven obeyed. He was just in time. Lance and Martin were standing uncertainly at the foot of the stairs, discussing the situation.

'D'you reckon I should go up and see if she's okay?' Martin was saying, sounding uncertain for once.

'I dunno,' said Lance. 'Maybe we oughta just split.'

'I only tried to kiss her,' said Martin.

Steven stopped in front of them.

'Well?' demanded Martin. 'What gives?'

Steven managed a light laugh. 'She's okay... she was just pulling your leg, is all.'

'Oh, what?' said Martin.

'Oh, what?' echoed Lance.

Steven gave a wintery smile. 'Yes, well, you did ask for it, Mr Expert. You're not exactly Valentino.'

Martin turned away. 'Well, if that's the way she's going to take it, we'll split,' he muttered.

'Hey, Martin,' said Lance. 'Who's this guy Valentino?'

'Great apes,' muttered Steven, when the boys had gone. He thought he'd convinced Martin and Lance, but he certainly hadn't convinced himself! He stood there uncertainly for a minute or two, punching one fist into the other palm, then turned and rushed back upstairs.

9

After Steven had left, Carly sobbed for a while, then sat up and blew her nose, shuddering with the effort of holding back more tears.

'It was that man, wasn't it?' asked Lynn. 'That man who gave you a lift?'

Carly nodded jerkily, twisting her handkerchief.

'I wish I'd gone with you, now,' said Lynn.

'No you don't,' corrected Carly flatly. That was so obviously true that Lynn got up and walked away.

'What'd he... you know... what'd he do?' asked Bobby.

Carly shuddered, but made an effort to be flip. 'Oh... the usual, I suppose, whatever that is...' The last word came out in a sob, and Lynn moved to go back to her. 'No, I'm okay,' said Carly.

Steven, arriving to hear this last statement, look disbelieving.

Carly blew her nose again and then spoke falteringly in a low voice. 'I sort of knew something was up when he turned into this dirt track and said it was a short-cut.

When he stopped, I tried to get away. I guess I made about twenty metres.'

'And that's when it happened?' said Bobby.

'Y-yes,' gasped Carly, and sobbed again.

Frank was attaching a gas bottle to another caravan when Martin and Lance passed by.

'Hey, Frankie!' called Martin. 'What've you been feeding your sister, eh? Looney pills?'

'What?' said Frank. He would have pursued this, but just then Tom's car drew up.

'Hey, Frank, sorry to leave you with those bottles,' said Tom. 'Something urgent came up.'

'Yeah?' Frank was only half-listening, still staring after Lance and Martin. If anyone had been at the looney pills, it was those two, he thought.

'Can you keep a secret?' asked Tom. He was grinning, and it was evident that he was hugely pleased with himself.

'A secret? Course I can!' said Frank. 'I mean to say — do I *look* like Celia Stewart?'

Tom grinned appreciatively. Everyone knew Alf's sister was the biggest mouth in Summer Bay.

'What's this secret then?' asked Frank.

'Help me get some things out of the car,' said Tom, lowering his voice mysteriously.

'That's a secret?'

Tom punched him lightly on the shoulder. 'I've got a surprise for Pippa,' he explained, 'but I'll need all you kids onside to make it work out.'

72

'Look here, Carly, I still say you'd better go to the police,' said Steven.

'No,' said Carly.

'But if you don't do that,' argued Steven, 'how are they going to catch him?'

'Oh, what's the point,' said Carly wearily, 'I didn't get the numberplate or anything...'

'What sort of car was it?' asked Bobby.

'White — I think,' said Carly. 'Lightish, anyway.'

'You must have noticed what make it was,' urged Steven.

'Well I didn't. At first it didn't matter, and later... I was too busy trying to fight him off. Lynn, you saw him pick me up. What about you? Can you remember?'

Lynn shook her head. 'Not really,' she said. 'It was just a car.'

'Well how about the creep himself?' said Bobby. 'What was *he* like?'

Carly shivered. 'Just a guy,' she said hopelessly. 'Bit older than Frank, I suppose. He was wearing shades.'

'Clothes?' said Lynn.

'Jeans — shirt — I don't know! I never had that good a look at him. He was just an ordinary guy.'

'Doesn't sound too ordinary to me,' said Steven darkly. 'Well, what are you going to do?'

Carly slumped. 'He could be anywhere.' Her voice rose. 'Anyway, the cops'll never catch him, so there's no point telling them about it, is there? So we won't, okay? We're not going to tell anyone anything.'

'All right, I was only trying to help!' said Steven huffily.

73

They all jumped as feet sounded on the stairs and the door swung open.

'Hey, you guys,' said Frank cheerfully. 'You'll never guess what Tom's got lined up for Pippa!'

Bewildered by the silence, Frank looked around the room. He blinked, then tried an uneasy grin. 'Okay. Take two. And this time, don't all talk at once.' He spun round. 'Hey, you'll never guess what Tom's got lined up . . .'

Finally, the lack of reaction penetrated, and Frank ran down like a clockwork toy. He looked from one face to another: Carly, her eyes red and puffy; Bobby, glowering blackly; Lynn, almost in tears; Steven, stern and solemn.

'What's happened?' said Frank. 'Steven? You tell me.'

Steven looked across at Carly. She shrugged. 'Oh, tell him if you like. You will anyway,' she said, then added fiercely, 'but if you tell Tom and Pippa I'll kill you! Oh, what's the use? I've said all I'm going to say.' She turned round and lay face downward.

'Well?' said Frank.

'Well . . . Carly got . . . well, she went . . .'

'Bloody hell!' said Bobby. '*I'll* tell him.' She turned to Frank. 'You know Carly and Lynn went to see Nico at the home yesterday?'

Mystified, Frank nodded.

'Well,' said Bobby flatly, 'Carly got a lift back, see, and the guy raped her. That plain enough for you?'

Frank looked sick. It was altogether *too* plain.

Strangely, his first reaction was anger with Carly, for taking such a risk. For being so stupid. But he knew there was no use in saying anything about that now. He swallowed.

'I'd better go and find Pippa,' he said.

'*No!*' yelled Carly. 'I won't have Pippa knowing! *I won't!*'

'Oh, come on!' said Frank. 'This is no joke!'

'You're telling *me* that?' cried Carly. She flung herself over again and sobbed.

Lynn put her arms round her. 'All right, all right, we won't tell Pippa,' she soothed.

'C'mon, let's get out of here,' muttered Bobby. Appalled, Frank followed.

'We've *got* to tell them!' he said as they went downstairs.

'Look, it's *her* it was done to, so it's *her* business, okay?' said Bobby.

'It's not just her business,' countered Frank. 'We should have a family conference on it.'

'What good'd *that* do?' asked Bobby.

'It'd make her wake up to herself.'

'Listen,' said Bobby crossly, 'she doesn't want Tom and Pippa knowing.'

'Well I still say they should be told,' said Frank.

'Told what?' said Pippa's voice from the corner armchair where she was slumped.

'Er — Pippa,' said Frank.

75

'Didn't see you there,' said Bobby as lightly as she could.

'Obviously,' said Pippa dryly. She looked from one guilty face to the other. 'Is this a big secret I should prise out of you, or a little secret I should ignore?'

'Would you believe — a little one?' said Frank.

'Hmm,' said Pippa darkly. 'I don't know about that . . . maybe not. But if it isn't and you *do* have a conference, I hope you'll have the sense to bring me and Tom in on it.' She grinned at them wearily. 'I'm too tired to pry, anyway. Let's just say I trust you and leave it at that.'

'Great,' said Frank as easily as he could. 'I've got some stuff to do outside. Catch you later, Bob!'

'Anything *you* want to say?' Pippa asked Bobby as Frank banged the door shut.

'Ha! Tryin' to get it out of me while I'm alone, eh?' grinned Bobby.

'Not really,' said Pippa. 'Can't help being curious, though. Still — you *would* tell me if it was serious, wouldn't you?'

'Sure,' said Bobby.

Pippa leaned back.

'You feelin' a bit down?' asked Bobby.

'Just tired and sorry for myself,' said Pippa.

'I wouldn't be in your shoes for quids,' said Bobby frankly.

'Come now, you kids aren't that bad,' said Pippa.

'Not us,' said Bobby with a laugh. '*That* one.' She indicated Pippa's stomach. 'The one you're goin' to have. Now me, I'm never goin' to have kids.'

'That's what I said,' pointed out Pippa. 'And now look at me! Besides, where would the human race be if nobody had kids?'

'There'd be a hell of a lot less of us 'n' I reckon that wouldn't be too bad,' said Bobby. 'Look at Lance 'n' Martin — wish *their* mums had had the sense to keep their legs crossed! Catch you!'

She went out after Frank, grinning at Tom as he passed her. 'Serviettes,' muttered Tom.

'Pardon?' said Pippa.

'What are you doing home?' asked Tom.

'Lovely to see you too, darling,' cooed Pippa. 'I'd had enough. What do you need serviettes for?'

'Serviettes? I don't need serviettes!'

'But that's what you said,' persisted Pippa. 'Serviettes.'

'No, no, not serviettes,' said Tom.

'Well, what *did* you say then?'

Tom looked about for inspiration and found none. 'Serves you right,' he offered at last. 'That's what I said.'

'Serves who right? What does?' asked Pippa.

'Oh... ahhh... stupid Lance and Martin. One of their pranks backfired. Serves them right, I say. That the time? Gees, I've got a mountain to do round the place before tea. You stay here and have a rest, promise?'

'All right,' said Pippa, puzzled. Tom retreated.

'They're all nuts,' said Pippa plaintively. 'Frank and Bobby — Tom — as bad as Lance and Martin!'

Then she grinned. No-one could be as bad as Lance and Martin.

Worn out, Pippa remained where she was, and slipped into a half-doze, to wake with a jump some time later. Rattling sounds from the kitchen indicated that someone, at least, had begun preparations for dinner. Pippa hurried out and, seeing that Lynn, Bobby and Frank had the peeling, chopping and slicing under control, she began to lay the table.

'I'll finish that for you,' offered Steven.

'Thanks,' said Pippa. 'I'm sorry, I'm all behind like a lamb's tail tonight. Comes of having a snooze.'

'Do you good,' said Steven kindly. 'You poor old thing!'

'Cheeky!' Pippa pulled a face at him.

'Don't worry about it,' soothed Frank. 'Doesn't matter if we eat late.'

'It matters if we don't eat at all,' said Pippa. 'those vegies ought to be half-cooked by now. Where's Tom?'

'Oh, he thought he heard a noise outside,' said Lynn. 'I did too. Didn't you hear a noise, Bob?'

'Yeah, I reckon,' said Bobby.

Tom stuck his head in the door. 'Excuse me, darling,' he said to Pippa. 'Can you give me a hand for a tick?'

'What've you found?' she asked.

'There's a possum in one of the caravans,' said Tom. 'I'll need help to chase him out.'

78

'Can't Frank do it?'

'I promised to help Sal with her homework,' said Frank quickly.

'I thought she usually asked Steven?'

'Well, normally ... yes,' said Steven. 'But I'm helping Bobby tonight, eh Bob?'

Bobby nodded vigorously. 'He's the brain, remember. We sort of ration him out.'

'Come on,' broke in Tom. 'It won't take a minute.'

'Oh, all right,' said Pippa. 'Can you kids carry on in here?'

'Sure,' said Bobby.

'No problem,' said Lynn.

'Don't hurry back,' said Steven.

'Cool it, you guys!' said Tom. 'Come on, Pippa.'

'Oh — can't it wait until morning?'

'Ah,' said Frank with a broad grin. 'I reckon tonight's definitely better ... in this case.'

Behind Pippa's back, Tom made an expressive throat-cutting gesture. Frank raised his eyebrows.

'Come on,' said Tom. He ushered Pippa out into the darkness. 'This one over here,' he said, indicating the caravan farthest from the house.

'It would be,' said Pippa. She cocked her head. 'I can't hear anything. Are you sure there's a possum?'

'Don't worry, it's in there,' assured Tom.

'I'm not going in first,' muttered Pippa, so Tom went in ahead. There was the sound of a match striking, and

79

he bent to light two candles which were standing in readiness on the table.

Pippa's eyes widened as she took in the scene revealed in the candlelight. Flowers, wine, a wonderful meal for two ... 'Oh ... is this for us?' she asked inadequately.

Tom gave her a hug. 'Romantic dinner for two, just like the lady ordered,' he said with a flourishing bow.

'And I've been so grumpy!' said Pippa.

'Never!' said Tom gallantly, pulling out a chair. 'If the lady would like to take her seat, the evening awaits!'

10

Steven closed the door on Pippa and Tom. 'Talk about luck!' he said in a low voice. 'Tom's idea means we can have the house to ourselves all night!'

'Yeah,' said Frank. His grin had vanished as the door closed. 'Get Carly.'

'You think she'll listen to us?' asked Lynn anxiously.

'She's going to have to,' said Frank.

'Go on then,' said Bobby.

Frank hesitated, then began to climb the stairs. Bobby, Steven and Lynn sat down at the table.

'I hope this won't take too long,' said Bobby with a grimace. 'I've still got two hundred words of a Macbeth essay to write.'

'Here they come,' said Lynn, but it was only Frank who came back into the room.

'What's up?' said Bobby.

'She's coming down,' said Frank.

'How did you manage that?' asked Steven.

'Easy,' said Frank glumly, 'I didn't actually tell her we were having a meeting.'

'What did you tell her? Actually?' said Bobby.

'I said dinner was ready.'

'Good goin', Frankie, she'll love it,' said Bobby.

'Where's Tom and Pippa?' asked Carly. 'And who'll love what?'

'They're out,' said Lynn awkwardly.

'Oh, are they really?' said Carly suspiciously. 'Well then, excuse *me*!' She spun round and headed for the stairs again. Frank grabbed hold of her arm. Carly jerked away and glared at him.

'Who the hell do you think you are, Frank?' she stormed. 'Getting me down here — sitting up like a bloody jury!'

'We've got to do something,' said Frank firmly.

'Why?' demanded Carly.

'You expect us to just sit back and carry on like everything's normal? Someone tells me, "Oh, by the way, Frank — Carly was raped yesterday." And I'm supposed to think "Gee, that's bad luck?"'

'Yes,' said Carly.

'Well that's just not on. We mightn't always get along, but we're family, Carly. I want to get that guy. We're *going* to get that guy! You can't tell me you wouldn't want to see him caught?'

Carly bit her bottom lip and clenched her fists.

'We don't think telling the police would help very much,' said Lynn hurriedly.

'But how are they ever meant to catch him if no-one *tells* them what he's done?' exclaimed Frank. 'Look Carly, if no-one says anything, he could do the same

82

thing to any number of girls. Is that what you want?'

She was silent.

'Well?' said Frank. 'Is it?'

'All I want ... please...' said Carly in a shaking voice, 'is to forget all about it. I don't want to be put on a guilt trip for not saying anything... I don't want revenge... I don't want everyone knowing about it and talking about it and saying I probably asked for it and it never would have happened if I hadn't got in the car. All I want... is for all of you... to help me forget.'

'You ought to go to the doctor, at least,' said Frank.

'What for?' flashed Carly. 'I've got a few bruises, okay. They'd only give me a lecture and poke me about — they can't do anything to make it better! Look, I'm going to bed.'

'At the very least,' said Frank stubbornly, 'I think we ought to tell Tom and Pippa.'

'Yeah,' said Steven.

'No!' said Carly.

'Carly...' said Frank, putting a hand on her arm. She flinched. 'Oh — sorry.'

'No!!! Can't you just forget it? It was *me* it happened to, not *you*! Don't I have *any* say in this?'

'I think it's too big for us to handle alone,' said Frank. 'You're gonna *need* Tom and Pippa, Carls... better we tell 'em now, eh?'

'No,' said Carly.

'Carly... stay and talk it over.'

'I'll see you in the morning,' said Carly distantly.

'You go upstairs,' threatened Frank, 'and I'm going out to Tom and Pippa right now!'

Carly turned back. 'Oh, that's fair,' she snapped. 'That's real fair. What're you going to do? Keep us here till we all agree with you? Some meeting!'

'All right!' said Frank. 'Let's have a vote then.'

'What?' said Carly. 'You're crazy!'

'That's what we do, isn't it?' hurried on Frank. 'Vote on important issues? Well, if you don't want me going straight to Tom and Pippa, we'll take a vote. See what the majority thinks.'

'You rat!' said Carly.

Frank stared at her inflexibly. 'Steven?' he said.

'I think we should tell them,' said Steven. 'I've thought so all along.'

'Lynn?'

Lynn exchanged glances with Carly, and wavered. 'No,' she said at last.

'Looks like it's up to you, Bob,' said Frank confidently. Bobby and Carly had never been known to agree on anything.

Bobby frowned. 'This is crazy,' she said. '*She* was the one it was done to. Not you, me or anyone else.'

'If we *don't* tell, it *will* be someone else,' said Frank. 'Well? Is that a yes or a no?'

'It's a no,' said Bobby. 'If she doesn't want us tellin' 'em, we shouldn't tell 'em.'

'What if it's you next time?' asked Frank.

Bobby glowered. 'Listen, I won't be hitchin', okay?' she said.

Despite this slightly sour note, Carly was grateful for Bobby's support. 'Thanks, Bob,' she said. 'And now, I'm going to my room. That's if nobody's got any more objections?'

Frank had plenty, but he didn't say so. The smell of burning vegetables suddenly alerted them, and as Lynn and Steven rushed to rescue the dinner, Carly slipped away upstairs, passing Sally on her way down.

'Where's Pippa?' asked Sally as she reached the bottom, 'and what's the matter with Carly? Oh, and what's that *smell*?'

Dinner tasted terrible, but nobody except Sally complained. It was a silent meal. Frank was sunk into an angry depression. Despite the family law that the majority vote carried the day, he knew it was all wrong. Carly's feelings deserved consideration, surely, but sometimes principles were more important than feelings, and Frank was certain that this was one of those times.

So Carly wanted them all to act as if nothing had happened? Well, he thought bitterly, how long was it going to be before Carly herself could do that? He hadn't missed the way she'd flinched when he'd just taken hold of her arm, and as for the way she'd gone berserk when Martin kissed her...!

Nobody felt much like conversation that evening, so Frank took himself off to his room early, leaving Bobby and Steven struggling with their homework while Lynn saw Sally into bed. Maybe things would look better tomorrow.

Unfortunately, they didn't. Frank went to work before

the others left for school, but for all he achieved, he might as well have stayed at home.

Carly didn't have a brilliant day, either. It wasn't improved when their school netball team was soundly thrashed in the first match of the season.

'Great start to the season, eh?' said Bobby as they went to their lockers. 'Done by twenty points!'

Carly shrugged.

'It was that beanpole Goal Shooter they had,' grumbled Bobby. 'All she had to do was reach up 'n' drop 'em in!'

Matt came up behind them. 'Hear you lost,' he said.

'Word travels fast,' said Bobby acidly, with one eye on Carly. What if Carly blew her top again with Matt?

'Who are you playin' next week?' he asked.

'I think it's Burton High,' said Carly.

'Ah, you'll kill *them*,' said Matt confidently. 'Love your knobbly knees, Bob!'

'Get outta here!' yelled Bobby, and chased him away.

'Why'd you vote for me, last night?' asked Carly offhandedly, as she came back.

''Cos I wanted your crib notes, of course!' said Bobby. 'I still haven't finished that essay for Fisher.'

Carly looked sceptical.

'Look,' said Bobby more softly, 'it's like this, Carls. If you weren't ready to face it, I wasn't gonna push you.'

'Thanks,' said Carly. She scuffed at the ground with one shoe. 'Hell of a way to lose it.'

'What?' asked Bobby, taken by surprise.

Carly looked at her pityingly. '*It*!'

'Oh.' said Bobby. 'You were a virgin, huh?'

'Just 'cos I like guys doesn't mean I ever...' said Carly.

'No... 'course not,' said Bobby. 'Just surprised, that's all.'

'If anyone ever finds out, I don't know what I'd do.'

'Relax,' said Bobby. 'No-one's gonna.'

Carly moved away, as if sorry she'd said so much.

Frank was still depressed when he reached home that afternoon and found Steven already at the table, studying.

Steven looked up casually as Frank came in. 'Hi, how was work?' he said.

'So-so,' said Frank. Steven looked at his set face and wisely went back to his books. 'How long're you going to be doing that?' asked Frank aggressively.

'A while,' said Steven.

Frank stalked over to where his guitar case was propped up. He settled on the couch and began playing monotonously.

'How long are *you* going to be doing *that*?' said Steven pointedly.

'Long as I feel like it,' said Frank.

'I get it,' said Steven, closing his book. 'Until you get all that stuff about Carly out of your system, right?'

Frank played a crashing chord, and then clapped his palm over the strings.

'We're *supposed* to be acting as though nothing's happened,' reminded Steven.

'I keep thinkin',' said Frank. 'How do we know he's not livin' right here at Summer Bay? If she could even've told us what he looked like...'

'We took a vote,' said Steven. 'It was your idea.'

'Well I thought Bobby'd go along with me, didn't I?'

'She didn't though,' pointed out Steven.

'Brilliant,' said Frank.

'She's a girl...'

'Really?'

'So,' continued Steven, 'she'd understand more about how Carly feels...'

'What's wrong with Carly?' enquired Sally, coming in with her dog bouncing behind her. 'Is she sick?'

Frank gathered up his guitar and went upstairs.

'What's wrong with her?' repeated Sally.

'Nothing, Sal. She's fine,' said Steven, and went back to his books.

11

Pippa and Tom seemed cheerful and relaxed after their evening alone, so Frank struggled to lighten his own mood. At dinner time, he helped Steven lay the table. 'Where's Carly?' he said as softly as possible.'

'Having a shower,' said Steven.

'Still?'

'I'm starvin',' announced Bobby, coming in from her van. 'What's on the menu?'

'Curry,' said Tom with a grin, bearing in a steaming dish. 'Extra hot. The lid came off while Pippa was putting it in.'

'Yuk,' said Bobby. 'Hope there's plenty of water?'

'A jugful,' put in Pippa. 'Are we all here?'

'Nearly,' said Frank.

'Full house,' said Tom, as Carly came down from upstairs. 'Ah, better cut your shower time, love, or you'll run us out of hot water. You seem to live in there, these days!'

Carly's face tightened, but she nodded.

'You haven't told us yet how the game went,' said Pippa, ladling out curry.

'We lost,' said Carly shortly.

'Massacred, more like it,' said Bobby. 'Thirty-two to twelve!'

'They're the top team,' said Steven excusingly, 'Sandra said they won the pennant last year.'

Bobby grinned. 'Oooh, been seein' sexy Sandy, have ya?'

'We're in the same class,' said Steven distantly.

'Just good friends... right?' said Tom, pacifically.

Steven grinned lamely. 'She's okay.'

'Are you all right now, Carly?' piped up Sally, mashing her potato into the curry.

Carly looked up. 'Yeah, I'm fine. Okay?'

'Steven said you weren't feeling good,' explained Sally.

'When?' said Steven.

'After school,' said Sally confidently. 'I heard you telling Frank that Carly was feeling bad. That's what he said, wasn't it, Frank?'

Frank shrugged. 'Can't remember.'

'He did,' said Sally firmly. 'He said...'

'Carly's already said she's fine,' said Tom, trying to quell any further argument. Tom liked meals to be peaceful.

'Then why isn't she like normal?' asked Sally.

Faces swivelled to look at Carly.

She shrugged. 'I'm tired after the game, that's all.'

'You might have a temperature,' said Sally hopefully. 'You might have a cold. Have you got a tummy ache?'

'Stop playing doctor,' said Tom firmly. 'If we need a medical opinion we'll ask Nurse Fletcher.'

Pippa looked across at Carly. 'You do look a bit run-down, love,' she said. 'Feeling okay?'

'I'm fine,' muttered Carly.

'She looks okay to me,' put in Bobby determinedly. 'Whaddya reckon, Frank?'

Frank studied his plate. 'Yeah ... s'pose.'

Carly looked at Sally. 'Satisfied?'

Alerted by her sullen tone, Pippa looked at her again. 'Been sleeping okay?' she asked.

'I've been sleeping fine.' Carly was beginning to feel cornered. 'Stop making such a hassle out of it.'

'It's not a hassle,' said Pippa mildly. 'I just asked ...'

Carly's voice slid up. 'Listen! I don't want to talk about it, okay?' she cried.

'Hey, come on!' said Tom, trying to smooth things down. 'She only asked you a question.'

Carly looked stoney.

'Frank?' Tom indicated Frank's plate. As he served up, Carly suddenly got up and went out.

Lynn rose to her feet. 'Lynn,' said Tom firmly. 'Sit down.'

'But, Carly ...'

'I'll talk to Carly later. Right now, you sit down and eat your dinner.'

Reluctantly, Lynn subsided.

Nobody really enjoyed dinner that night, and it wasn't only due to the overdose of curry powder!

'You could have been a bit more convincing,' said

91

Bobby reproachfully to Frank as they did the washing up.

'What'd you expect me do?' he asked. 'Get up on the table and dance?'

'Something, anyway. Anyone'd think you *wanted* them to twig.'

'P'r'aps I do,' said Frank under his breath.

Tom came through with a couple of plates. 'I thought Carly was on kitchen tonight?' he said.

Bobby shrugged. 'I s'pose . . . oh well, it's no hassle.'

'Carly slides out on her turn and there's no complaint? Whose leg are you pulling?'

'She can pay us back later,' said Bobby. 'Double, if you like.'

'She probably *is* a bit crook,' said Frank.

'She *said* she was okay!' said Bobby angrily.

'Yeah I know. It's just that she's been a bit edgy . . .'

'You're right there,' said Tom.

'Look, if it's such a big deal I'll go 'n' get her.'

'No, it's all right,' said Tom thoughtfully. 'I'll go. Wouldn't mind a bit of a chat.'

'What the hell did you say that for?' snapped Bobby when Tom had gone.

Frank looked sulky. 'I wanna make sure they get the creep who did it, okay?'

'Oh yeah . . . and what do you think's goin' to happen to Carly then, eh? Coupla days in court with some nice lawyers? Few harmless little questions? Smiles all round . . . the bloke's chucked in the slammer, and bingo, it's all over and everything's fine? Blimey! You're thicker than I thought!'

Steven looked up from where he was making himself a hot drink. 'So much for the family vote,' he said.

Carly was sitting blindly in front of the mirror, brushing her hair, as Tom tapped on the door. In a dull haze of misery, she barely noticed the sound.

Tom poked his head round the door. 'Carly? Can I come in?'

'If you're worried about the washing up,' said Carly listlessly, 'I'll do it tomorrow. Bob doesn't mind.'

'So she says,' said Tom. 'But it's you I'm worried about tonight.'

'I told you, I'm fine!' said Carly.

Tom came over and sat next to her, putting a hand on her shoulder. 'Love, if there's anything the matter, you can tell me . . .' he began.

Carly flinched and moved away, putting down her brush and picking up her copy of *Macbeth*.

'I'm not going to bite your head off, you know,' said Tom. 'But there's one thing I've always been proud of in our family: the way we can talk to one another.'

'We're meant to hand in an essay on this tomorrow,' said Carly.

Tom disregarded this. 'Frank seems to think you might be a bit tense over something.'

'I bet he does,' muttered Carly.

'Are you?' said Tom directly.

'Why do they keep teaching Shakespeare, anyway?' said Carly desperately.

'Carly...'

'It's irrelevant!' said Carly angrily. 'They should teach stuff about what *we* have to go through. Not some stupid rubbish about witches and kings!'

'Carly, what's wrong?'

Carly turned on him, clutching *Macbeth* to her chest like a shield.

'You keep asking me what's wrong. *That's* what's wrong!' she cried. 'I didn't *ask* you to come and talk to me, did I? You and Pippa — you're always doing that! As soon as anyone stops smiling for a coupla minutes, you have to ask them what's wrong! I'm *sick* of it!'

'Is that it?' said Tom quietly.

Carly nodded.

'All right, I'll leave you alone then,' said Tom. 'Okay?'

Carly's throat ached. 'Okay,' she managed.

Tom went out and quietly closed the door. He stood there uncertainly for a moment, and then went down the stairs to where the other kids were waiting nervously in the kitchen.

'I'm just going for a walk, okay?' he said, and went out.

'D'you think he knows?' asked Frank.

'Not your fault if he doesn't,' said Bobby, and stalked out to her van.

When Lynn went up to bed, Carly was asleep — or pretending to be, which amounted to the same thing.

Steven caught up with Carly outside her locker the next morning at school.

'What'd Tom say to you?' he asked in a low voice.

'The usual,' said Carly. 'Talk, talk, talk, that's all he knows.'

'You didn't tell him?'

'What d'*you* reckon? Frank's going to keep at it till one of 'em twigs though, if I can't shut him up. Last night was just the start.'

'I'll talk to him, okay?' said Steven. 'How'd you do with the essay?'

'I filled a few pages. Can't remember what I wrote. Look, there's the bell. See ya.'

'Keep it together, eh?' said Steven.

He went away to his first class. Carly, turning away from her locker, caught sight of Bobby talking confidentially to two of their classmates, Matt and Alison. Alison was looking in her direction.

Carly marched over towards them, just as Matt and Alison left Bobby and headed for their first class.

'Thanks a lot,' she said flatly as she came up to Bobby.

'What's that s'posed to mean?' asked Bobby in an injured voice.

'Just couldn't wait to tell everybody, could you?'

'What?'

'What do you think?' asked Carly sarcastically. 'I'm not blind. I saw that Alison looking at me as if I was some sort of freak or something!'

'Not *you*, you berk, *Steven*!' said Bobby.

'*Steven*!'

'I was only tellin' them how Steve was startin' to come on to Sandy Barlow,' said Bobby defensively. 'Why don't you ask 'em?'

'Okay, okay. So I made a mistake. Sorry.'

'You made a mistake all right!' said Bobby. 'We're bustin' a gut to cover for ya, and you're walkin' round like paranoid zombie!'

'Look, I *said* I was sorry,' said Carly.

'Well — we'd best be goin'. Fisher's waitin'.'

Fisher was indeed waiting. Soon after the class began he started hassling Bobby.

'I'm waiting, Simpson!' he snapped, as Bobby hesitated on an answer.

'What for, sir?' Bobby was all innocence.

'For a coherent answer,' said Fisher heavily. 'Now, if Lady Macbeth's the power behind the throne, how did she use this power over Macbeth?'

Bobby bit the end of her ballpoint, and considered, 'Well, he was a wimp, wasn't he?' she said.

'A wimp?' said Fisher terribly.

'Yeah. He was scared of ghosts.'

Fisher raised hands and eyes to heaven, but Bobby hadn't finished yet. 'And he believed all that gnat's eyes and bat's tooth stuff, eh?'

Fisher breathed deeply. 'But how did Lady Macbeth exercise her power? Who'd like to enlighten her? You, perhaps Morris?'

Carly was doodling on her folder, and didn't react.

'Morris?' repeated Fisher.

'Mmm?' Carly looked up.

'Well?' demanded Fisher.

'Um . . . I didn't hear the question, sir.'

'I'm not surprised,' said Fisher, looming. 'English class is for English, not doodling.'

'Yes, sir.'

Fisher glared at Carly for a few moments more, and then paced on. 'The idea of women controlling men is not new,' he continued. 'Let's face it, a man is usually no match for a woman determined to get her own way.'

'Garbage,' said Carly bitterly.

'I beg your pardon, Morris? I believe you spoke? Perhaps you'd like to share your valuable opinion with the class?'

'What you just said, about women. It's . . .'

'Hey sir!' interrupted Bobby, anxious to take the heat off Carly. 'What was the witches' prophecy all about, anyway?'

'See me in my office, after class,' said Fisher to Carly, and, to the rest of the class, 'I want all those essays now, please. Hand them to the front.'

12

The lecture from Fisher was sharp and brief, and made briefer by the fact that it was interrupted by the sudden arrival of the Head, Mr Bertram.

'Hello, sir, how are you feeling?' said Carly, pleased to see him for more than one reason.

'Fine, fine,' said Bertram. 'Not interrupting anything, Donald, I trust?'

'She was just leaving,' said Fisher heavily. Carly took the hint and left for her next class, which was, in its turn, interrupted by an official announcement of Mr Bertram's return.

Judging by the spontaneous cheers which broke out, this was very popular news!

'Did ya check the look on Fisher's face when he came in for this arvo?' gloated Bobby as they walked home from school. 'He'll have to pull his horns in now — Bertram's back! Let's party!' She whooped, unusually cheerful.

'What's the matter?' asked Sally as they entered the caravan park. Bobby explained, but Sally wasn't very interested in Fisher and his woes, and lost interest. 'Are you still sick, Carly?' she asked.

'No,' said Carly shortly.

'Hey!' said Steven. 'I'm going for a swim. Wanna come?'

'Good thinkin',' said Bobby with slightly forced enthusiasm. 'What about it, Carls?'

Carly shook her head. 'Oh well...' said Bobby. 'P'r'aps not. Think I'll pass too, Steve.'

'Okay,' said Steven, and went on ahead with Sally.

Bobby turned to Carly. 'Don't smile too much,' she advised. 'Your face might crack!'

'You don't let up, do you!' complained Carly as she followed Bobby into the house.

'Well, I'm gettin' sick of this. You say you wanna forget, so we all try to act normal, and all you can do is jump down me throat! Look, are you gonna sharpen up your act, or not?'

'I'm trying, okay?'

'You call bitin' everyone's head off and then gettin' hauled up in front of Flathead, tryin'? Eh?'

Carly shrugged.

'Havin' second thoughts?' said Bobby. 'That it?'

'What about?' Carly was suspicious.

'Tellin' the cops.'

'No! You think it's so easy, don't you? You think I can just laugh and smile, just like that, just like it never happened?'

'Look,' said Bobby more gently. 'You said you wanted us to help you forget. That's what I'm tryin' to do. But look, if it's too much for you . . .: if you just *can't* get it out of your mind . . . maybe you really oughta tell Tom and Pippa.'

No answer. Bobby sighed. She hadn't really expected one. 'Think about it,' she advised. 'You've gotta find some way of handlin' it, or you'll end up a nut case.'

'I can handle it, I can handle it! Okay? Now get off my back!' flashed Carly, and terminated the conversation by going upstairs.

With a lot of support from the others, Carly made it through that evening undetected, but she thought Tom had looked at her oddly once or twice.

She had a bad night, and woke more than once with a gasp and a sob, but as light began to creep in through the window, she made up her mind. Bobby had a point. She must make an effort — at least around Tom and Pippa.

She waited until she heard Tom moving around in the kitchen, cutting his lunch for work, and then put on her dressing gown and slipped downstairs.

'Hi, Tom!' she said breezily.

'Morning,' said Tom. He smiled at her guardedly.

'Oh, I was going to fix your lunch for you this morning,' said Carly.

'Thanks anyway, love, got to rush . . .'

'I'm sorry,' said Carly. 'About the other night, I mean. It's just that Fisher's been getting at me, and we lost our first netball match, and ... well, you know what it's like? How everything just gets on top of you sometimes? It makes you feel like dumping on someone else.'

'Yeah,' said Tom, and smiled more openly. 'Well, maybe I ought to be doing the apologising, for nagging at you. See you tonight, love.'

'See you!' said Carly. She held her cheery smile and attitude until Tom had gone out and then sagged into a chair. She sat there for a few moments until movement upstairs alerted her. She got up and went slowly back upstairs. She wouldn't go to school today.

Some time later, when the house was quiet again, Carly came down dressed for a day at the beach. Frank was alone in the dining area. 'Takin' the day off school, eh?' he said.

Carly ignored him.

Frank sighed. 'What have I done now?'

Carly rounded on him. 'You're a lousy loser. You should stick by the vote.'

'I have,' said Frank.

'To the letter, maybe, but you've been stirring. Trying to make Tom see there's something wrong.'

'I still say he should be told,' said Frank stubbornly.

'Says you,' said Carly.

'Well look,' said Frank. 'If you ever do change your

102

mind, and want to get the guy... I don't mean now, but sometime... just tell me, okay? I'll be first in line.'

'I won't need any help,' said Carly in an odd tight voice.

'Eh?' Frank was startled.

'I want to forget it, forget him, never think of it again. Because you know something? If I ever see his face again, the way I feel now... I'd kill him. I'd just kill him!'

Frank was startled and almost shocked. This was heavy stuff, and he didn't know that he could deal with it. Before he could comment, Carly had grabbed up her towel and slipped out. He might have followed, but the telephone was shrilling its summons.

'Yes?' he said, lifting the receiver.

'Frank? That you, love?' said a familiar husky voice. 'It's Floss McPhee here... Listen, love, can I speak to Nev?'

Neville came to the phone with rather bad grace: he was still annoyed with Floss about the stand she had taken over their grandson. He was even sourer when he heard what Floss had to say.

'We're gettin' on real well, him an' me,' she claimed contentedly.

'You're getting too involved,' said Neville shortly.

'Yeah, but if you'd seen the look on the poor little tyke's face after that phone call...'

'Floss...'

'He was heartbroken... he's just a lonely little boy, really. Look at the Fletcher lot. Happy as larks...

103

Tom 'n' Pippa carin' for 'em like they were their own...'

'Careful, Floss. You'll get in over your head if you're not careful.'

'I already am in over me head,' said Floss. 'I wish you'd come an' meet him, Nev. I really wish you would,'

'No,' said Neville.

'Well, if you won't meet him here, I'll bring him to Summer Bay.'

'Have you gone mad?'

'Just a coupla days. Country air... outdoor livin'... do him the world of good. I mean it, Nev.'

'No!' said Neville again. 'Absolutely, En Oh. NO! And that's final.' He put down the phone hastily, and turned to Frank. 'The woman's gone mad!' he said with real dismay. 'Wants to bring the kid to Summer Bay! I told her no way, but she's going to do it! You should have heard her, Frank, holding you lot up as an example.' He pitched his voice higher, mimicking Floss: '"Happy as larks, those Fletcher kids... Tom and Pippa carin' for them like their own!"'

Still upset, he shook his head to Frank's offer of coffee and went away.

Frank went on with what he had been doing. Happy as larks, were they? Well if they weren't it wasn't the fault of Pippa and Tom. Some things, reflected Frank moodily, even the best of parents couldn't prevent.

●

Lynn was finding out much the same thing. Ever since the accident to Nico Pappas, she had felt as a boat might feel when the anchor is cut away. Lynn's faith had always been her anchor, her assurance that, whatever happened, she would come through. But Nico's illness had finished all that.

What had poor Nico ever done to deserve what had happened to him? First, the determined persecution of Fisher, then the vilification by the locals who were willing to be convinced by Fisher that Nico was the dangerous local nutter. And then the nutter had struck at Nico himself . . . poisoning his beloved cow. Nico's grip on reality had never been very strong, and that was enough to strain it severely. He had retreated into what was almost a state of coma. And why? What harm had Nico ever done to anyone?

No wonder Lynn's faith had been almost as stressed as Nico's mind. And then, after the successful visit to the mental home, just as she was beginning to feel that things weren't entirely black, it had happened again. This time to Carly. All right, Carly shouldn't have been hitch-hiking.

But it wasn't fair! clamoured Lynn's mind. Why should she suffer so much for such a little thing? And why should that man — that creature — drive off scot-free while Carly suffered and, in suffering, rocked the stability of the family?

So Lynn, frightened and unhappy, retreated into her depression, and resisted every attempt by kind Father Rawlings, the local priest, to draw her into any

discussions about her drifting state. And Father
Rawlings was persistent. He even visited Tom and
asked him to help. Tom had replied, characteristically,
that religious conviction, or lack of it, was up to the
individual, but he did agree to make an opportunity
for Lynn to talk if she wished.

Lynn hadn't wished. She firmly refused all
discussion on the subject, and left the house.

It was pure bad luck that she met Celia Stewart that
morning. It was even worse luck that Celia happened
to be rallying support for the imminent church fete.
And it was the worst luck of all that Celia was the
biggest mouth in Summer Bay.

The situation was a time bomb, and the scene set for
a very big bang indeed.

13

They met on the road.

Lynn would have passed by with a mere flick of a wave by way of acknowledgement, but Celia, with the self-satisfied smile of the righteous, flagged her down. Reluctantly, Lynn pulled over to the side of the road, and put one foot on the road, keeping the other on her pedal for a quick getaway when the opportunity arrived. 'And how are we feeling today?' asked Celia with an arch cosiness that put Lynn's teeth on edge.

'Fine, Miss Stewart,' she answered politely.

'You know about our fete, I take it?' said Celia.

Lynn admitted that she did.

'Then we can expect you along . . . to help, perhaps?' prompted Celia.

'I can't Miss Stewart. Sorry, but I'm busy.'

'Oh, that's a shame,' said Celia.

Lynn shifted her balancing foot, but Celia didn't take the hint. 'Can I get past, please?' said Lynn rather sharply.

'Well, I was hoping for a brief word, actually,' said Celia.

Lynn sighed, and glanced ostentatiously at her watch, indicating that it had better be brief.

Celia licked her lips and plunged. 'I was hoping, perhaps, that you'd like to come along to one of our prayer meetings,' she said.

'I don't believe in prayer meetings any more,' said Lynn curtly. 'Now, can I get past, please?'

Gamely, Celia refused to look shocked. 'Perhaps you should visit the Reverend,' she said. 'I know you're the other... colour, for the moment... but I'm sure he'll be more than happy to talk to you.'

'I don't want to visit anyone and I don't want to be talked to,' said Lynn angrily. 'Now, I've got to go. I'm going to be late for school!'

'Don't you think,' said Celia seriously, 'that you're carrying this loss of faith thing a little far? In my opinion there's a lot to be said for moderation.'

'Miss Stewart, I've already said I...'

'I'm sure if you just come along to one of our prayer meetings,' said Celia stubbornly, 'you'd see things in a much clearer light.'

The tight feeling in Lynn's head seemed to explode. 'I don't care about your stupid meetings!' she cried hysterically. 'If there is a God, I hate him!'

'Lynn!' exclaimed Celia. 'How dare you?'

'Well, why shouldn't I?' demanded Lynn. 'He let my dog Eric get poisoned, let Nico's cow get poisoned, let Nico get put in that hospital, let Carly go hitch-hiking and get raped — ' She gasped, and stopped short, then barged past Celia and pedalled away.

The time bomb had gone off.

Lynn rode frantically, her ears still ringing with what she'd said. And to Celia Stewart, of all people!

Ahead of her, Carly and Bobby were just entering the school gates, arguing about the biology assignment. As Lynn skidded to a halt, Carly snapped something and quickened her pace.

'Bobby!' gasped Lynn.

Bobby was diverted from whatever Carly had said and turned back to Lynn. 'Yeah? What's up?'

'I told her ... Bobby! I *told* her!' wailed Lynn.

'Hold on, hold on,' said Bobby. 'Now, what are you talkin' about? Told who what?'

'Celia!' cried Lynn tragically.

'Hey, calm down. Now. What are you talkin' about?'

'I couldn't help it!' said Lynn. 'She started going on and on about God and why didn't I go to church any more and wouldn't I like to go to one of her horrible prayer meetings ...'

'Lynn ...' said Bobby warningly. 'What's all this about?

'I told her about Carly!' admitted Lynn in a small voice.

'You didn't? Oh, no! You dillbrain!'

'I couldn't help it,' pleaded Lynn.

'Oh, hell. But to tell Celia Stewart — why didn't you just print an ad in the paper? Motormouth'll have it all over town by lunchtime.'

'I know,' said Lynn. 'Carly's gonna kill me.' Drooping, she began to push her bike towards the school.

'Hang on . . .' interrupted Bobby.

'I have to tell her though.'

Bobby was thinking hard. 'Yeah, well we mightn't have to,' she said slowly. 'I've got an idea.'

'Oh, what?' said Lynn. She looked so hopeful that Bobby made up her mind. 'Look. I'm going over to Alf Stewart's. You go on into school and *don't worry*. Catch you later! Oh, and Lynn . . .'

'Yeah?'

'Lend me your bike, eh?'

Lynn thrust it towards her. Bobby mounted and shot out of the schoolyard.

It wasn't far to Alf's liquor store, and Bobby practically broke the speed limit to get there. Fortunately, there were no customers, and when Alf realised that Bobby wasn't there merely for a chat, he took her into the back room.

Tersely, Bobby told him what had happened to Carly. 'And now Lynn's gone and let it out to your sister,' she ended.

'You're jokin'!' said Alf. He didn't need to be told what a disaster *that* was.

'It's the truth,' said Bobby.

'The rotten mongrel! Just a minute, I'll phone up and get on to Celia right now . . . listen, does Carly know who he was? Was he a local bloke?'

110

Bobby shrugged. 'She'd never seen him before. She was just hitch- hikin' back from the home Nico's in and he picked her up.'

'Hitch-hiking!' groaned Alf. 'Don't you kids ever flamin' learn?' He frowned at the telephone and hung up. 'Engaged,' he said sourly.

Bobby sagged. 'Oh, great,' she muttered. 'That means she's probably blabbing it all over town right now...'

Alf reached out to the hook where he kept his car keys. 'Yeah, well you get back to school, Bobby,' he said. 'I'll take care of Celia.'

'Thanks,' said Bobby. She wished Alf had taken care of Celia years ago. Permanently.

'Of course, you know Carly should have gone to Tom and Pippa in the first place,' said Alf.

'I know,' said Bobby. 'But she thought the best way to get over it was to keep quiet...'

'Yeah, you kids think you know it all,' complained Alf. He was thinking of his own daughter. 'But look, this sort of think has got to be handled by adults.'

Bobby gave him a challenging look. 'Yeah?' she drawled. 'Don't forget, it was an adult who did it to her in the first place...' She turned away.

'Cheeky young beggar...' commented Alf, but he looked thoughtful as he locked up the store and got in his car.

Naturally Celia had not been able to keep such a choice bit of news to herself. When Alf turned into her

111

driveway she was leaning avidly over the fence talking to her next-door neighbour, Margaret.

'You expect that sort of thing in the city, don't you,' she said confidentially. 'I mean, you only have to watch the news... But not in Summer Bay!'

'Too many outsiders moving in, that's what I say,' said Margaret, in the truculent tones of one who had been born in Summer Bay.

'Well...' Celia dropped her voice. 'You *do* have to ask yourself... what sort of girl goes hitch-hiking...' She became aware that Margaret's attention had wandered and she was looking beyond Celia's head into the driveway.

'It's your brother,' said Margaret.

'I wonder what he wants?' said Celia, diverted.

Alf strode up. 'G'day, Maggie — see you later, eh?' he said.

'Well, pardon me for interrupting...' said Margaret, offended.

'Alfred!' exclaimed Celia.

Alf stopped her with a sharp wave of his hand. 'Who have you told about Carly Fletcher?'

'I've no idea what you're talking about!' said Celia grandly.

'I bet,' said Alf, 'You couldn't pass up a piece of gossip like that if your life depended on it!'

'That's a terrible thing to say!' exclaimed Celia, wounded.

'Never mind the indignation routine... who have you told?'

112

'Well . . . Margaret,' admitted Celia.

'And who else? I tried to ring, but your phone was running hot. So help me, Celia, if you've blabbed all over town . . .'

'Margaret and Doris Peters,' said Celia defensively. 'That's all, I swear.'

'Doris Peters!' moaned Alf.

'She promised not to tell anyone.'

'Yeah,' said Alf darkly. 'And everyone *she* tells will promise not to tell either. You know what you bunch of harpies have done? Do you? That poor kid won't be able to go anywhere without people sniggering behind her back. I always said that tongue of yours would do some real damage one day! Well, you've been 'n' gone 'n' done it now, and I hope you're happy!'

Alf stalked back to his car and went round to the school. It was recess time, and Lynn and Bobby were hovering near the school gate. Bobby raised a hand, said something to Lynn and went over to the car.

'How'd you get on?' she asked.

'Not so good,' said Alf sadly. 'The old . . . er . . . Celia had already talked.'

'Damn!' Bobby screwed up her face. 'How many had she told?'

'Only two — ' said Alf, but they both knew that telling two was enough. 'I might've managed to muzzle Margaret,' he said reflectively, 'but you know that Doris Peters . . .'

Bobby sighed. She knew. Doris Peters was practically Celia's spiritual twin.

'The trouble is,' broke in Alf, 'that she doesn't *mean* any harm! She's just congenitally unable to keep her mouth shut, that's all.'

'That's enough,' said Bobby grumpily. 'Oh well, thanks anyway, Alf. You tried.'

She turned back to where Lynn was waiting anxiously, and shook her head.

Lynn's face fell.

'You know what we've gotta do?' said Bobby without enthusiasm.

'Yeah,' said Lynn. 'But look, Bob. This isn't your problem.'

'No?' said Bobby cynically. 'Come on, let's go and get her.'

She strode purposefully towards the school building, with Lynn trailing behind.

They found Carly in the corridor and shepherded her unceremoniously into an empty classroom.

'Now,' said Bobby firmly, cutting across Carly's flood of protest. 'We've got something to tell you — okay? And we don't want the others standin' around with their ears flappin'...'

Carly sat down on a desk and folded her arms. 'Well? What is it?'

'It's all my fault,' burst out Lynn.

Carly raised her eyebrows.

'Lynn told Celia what happened ... when you hitched back from the mental home,' said Bobby flatly.

114

'I didn't *mean* to!' cried Lynn.

'You *promised*!'

'It was an accident!'

Carly slid off the desk. 'Whaddya mean it was an *accident*? You don't tell something like that by *accident*! You have to open your stupid great mouth and do it!'

'It's no good tearin' into Lynn,' put in Bobby. 'That's not gonna solve anything...'

'Yeah?' cried Carly. 'What would you know? It's not you who was... Everybody'll know... I won't be able to go anywhere, I won't be able to do anything... Don't you understand? *Everyone*'ll know!'

'Half of 'em probably know already,' said Bobby.

'Whaaat?'

'Look, I tried. I went and saw Alf. He tried to muzzle the old bag, but it was already too late.'

'Oh, great. Thanks a lot, Lynn...'

'I'm sorry! I'm sorry!' cried Lynn, covering her face.

'All right, it's happened,' said Bobby. 'We're stuck with it. Thing is, now you've gotta tell Tom 'n' Pippa.'

Carly shook her head.

'Carly, you've *got* to,' insisted Bobby. 'You can't let them find out from someone else. You've got to tell them yourself. And quick.'

14

Finally, Carly had to agree. Telling Pippa and Tom would be difficult: the alternative would be impossible. She would talk to them at the first opportunity.

This was at lunchtime, and she was already too late.

Just before lunch Pippa had gone to Ailsa's store. As she entered, she registered the speculative gaze of the single customer. She nodded and the woman came up and smiled at her. 'Excuse me...?'

'Yes?' said Pippa.

'You're Mrs Fletcher, aren't you?'

'Yes, that's right.' Pippa was puzzled, trying to identify the other woman.

'I'm Colleen Smart.'

'Oh, of course,' said Pippa. 'You're Lance's mother.'

Mrs Smart looked gratified. 'That's right. I've been meaning to drop by and thank you for letting him stay at the caravan park... he got a bit too much for his dad and me. No real harm in him, of course, but you know how it is. These youngsters like to have their freedom.'

Pippa smiled non-committally.

117

'Mind, if he starts getting in your way you just turf him straight back home again,' said Mrs Smart vigorously. 'You've got enough on your plate without having *him* underfoot, causing trouble.'

Pippa frowned at her enquiringly. Despite occasional yearnings for peace and quiet with Tom, she had never considered the family as any sort of burden.

Mrs Smart clicked her tongue. 'I tell you, when I heard about it... mind you, he wouldn't be a local feller... though there's a few around here I wouldn't look sideways at... but nah, not something like that. Somebody passing through, I reckon.'

'I'm sorry? I don't think I quite follow you...' said Pippa.

'Now don't get me wrong,' ploughed on Mrs Smart. 'Lance says your Carly's a decent girl. You've only gotta look at how she sent Martin packing, and that was only a bit of fun. There's no way she asked for it, I don't care what anyone says. To my mind there's only one answer to a bloke who'd do anything like that... the old snip-snap, if you know what I mean.'

It was just as well she wasn't really expecting an answer, for Pippa's thoughts were moving far too quickly for speech.

When she added Carly's edginess over the last few days to what Mrs Smart had said, the sum made horrible sense.

'Not a local feller... your Carly's a decent girl... only one answer for a bloke who'd do a thing like that...'

Oh Carly! Oh no!

Mrs Smart had collected her shopping. 'Be seeing you then, Mrs Fletcher,' she said cheerfully. 'An' don't forget what I said. About Lance, I mean.'

No, Pippa wouldn't forget what she'd said. About anything.

She had stood there frozen for a couple of minutes when the door swung open and Carly, Bobby and Lynn hurried in. 'Pippa!' gasped Bobby. 'Got a sec? Somethin' we should talk about.'

Pippa looked at them rather blankly, and Carly's spirits drooped even more. It seemed that they, like Alf Stewart, were just too late.

There wasn't really time to talk then, for the girls had to go back to school, and even later, when they returned to the house, no-one quite knew what to say. Sally's presence made open discussion impossible anyway.

Finally, Tom and Pippa retired to the girls' room for a private interview with Carly. There was a phone call and much discussion, which ended in Tom taking Carly to the police station.

Bobby began to do her homework at the table. Steven had finished his, but Lynn couldn't even pretend. She stood at the window looking out into the darkness.

Finally, the car pulled up outside. Carly came straight in, and without looking at anyone, went up the stairs.

Tom went into the kitchen. Pippa followed, closing the door behind her.

'Tom?' she said questioningly.

Tom had his back to her and didn't immediately turn round. He spoke in a muffled voice. 'When did we stop being members of this family?'

'They thought they were helping her...' said Pippa quietly.

Tom turned to face her. 'Yeah, well all they've done is to muck it up. The sergeant says even if they caught the guy there'd be Buckley's hope of getting a conviction. This long after the event there wouldn't be any evidence... she should have got over there straight away. Seen a doctor before she even had a shower. She should have come to us... Why didn't she come to us?'

'I'm not sure the evidence is important right now,' suggested Pippa. 'And the chances were it wouldn't have helped anyway. It's not as if she was much knocked around. We'd have noticed if she had been...'

'It's just the thought of that creep running around loose!' burst out Tom. 'And even if they caught up with him, we couldn't do anything about it...'

'I know.'

'We got away from the city, came up here because it was supposed to be a good place to bring up kids... teach them the right values, give 'em a start... and now something like this has to happen! My God! Hasn't Carly been through enough, before she came to us? Her father kills her mum and puts her in hospital —

120

and now this! Pippa, what's it going to do to her? Oh, I feel like I want to strangle somebody — beat him to a pulp... They should have told us, Pip!'

'I know...' said Pippa. She put her arms around him. Carly wasn't the only one whose faith in human nature had been damaged.

Lynn turned away from the window at last, and went silently up the stairs after Carly. She knocked on the bedroom door and went in. 'Can I come in?' she asked.

'Looks like you already *are*,' said Carly.

'Was it awful?' ventured Lynn. 'At the police station, I mean?'

'What do *you* think?' snapped Carly.

Lynn shrank down.

'Oh — well no, it wasn't that bad,' said Carly after a while. 'The sergeant was okay. Gave me a bit of a lecture, that's all.'

'Oh, Carly!' gasped Lynn. 'I'm so sorry! I never meant...'

'Look, it's not your fault, okay?' said Carly impatiently. 'It was that big-mouth Celia Stewart. Always sticking her nose in where it isn't wanted...' Her voice trailed away as Pippa came in and smiled quickly at Lynn. 'Tom wants to see you downstairs, love,' she said.

Lynn took the hint and went away.

'He's really angry, isn't he?' said Carly in a low voice.

'Mmm. He's going to read the riot act to all of them I'm afraid,' said Pippa.

121

'And you're going to do the honours with *me*. Well, don't bother. I've heard it all: "Hitch-hiking's dumb... I'm lucky it wasn't worse... I could have been killed..."' Carly's voice wobbled.

'I'm not here to give you a lecture,' said Pippa. 'I just thought maybe you could do with some company. Look, Tom's worried sick about you: he thinks this episode might spoil your life ... ruin your trust in people. It's not going to do that, is it?'

Carly shrugged.

'Look,' said Pippa earnestly. 'It can only ruin your life if you let it. So you took a silly risk and met a thoroughly rotten man. He hurt you and frightened you and made you feel dirty and ashamed. Right?'

Carly put her hands over her face.

'But that — experience — that had nothing to do with you as a person,' continued Pippa. 'And you're still the same person now as you were before.'

'I'm not a virgin any more,' mumbled Carly.

'No,' said Pippa quietly. 'Not physically, anyway.'

Carly gave a little choke. 'Hell of a first time, wasn't it?'

'That wasn't a first time,' said Pippa. 'Not in the way you mean it. Carly — love — what happened to you had no more in common with normal love-making than a punch in the eye has with holding hands. It was violence, pure and simple. So, although you're right when you say hitch-hiking is dumb, there's really no more shame attaching to you than if you'd been bashed and robbed. Okay?'

122

'But, other people...' began Carly.

'No, other people won't always see it like that,' said Pippa honestly. 'You're frightened about what they're going to say about you, true?'

Carly nodded.

'Well anyone who says anything nasty — to you or about you — isn't worth worrying about. Believe me.'

'But it isn't you who has to face them, is it?' said Carly.

Pippa sighed ruefully. There was really no answer to that.

Tom's riot act was in full swing. He had rounded up Frank and Steven, Lynn and Bobby, and was letting them have both barrels.

'We're supposed to be family!' he exploded. 'How do you think Pippa and I feel being left in the dark about something as important as this? Pippa had to find out about it from a stranger! What do you think that did to her?'

'We were going to tell her...' ventured Lynn.

'Only because you knew we were going to find out anyway!' countered Tom. He turned on Frank. 'And you, Frank! You're the eldest! Hell, you're supposed to be an adult! I expected more sense out of you...'

'Frank and Steve wanted to tell you all along,' broke in Bobby. 'We outvoted them.'

'Oh, I see,' scoffed Tom. 'It doesn't matter what's right as long as you vote on it first, eh?'

'That's the way we always do it,' pointed out Lynn. 'Not with something like this!'

'It's not fair giving them a hard time,' said Carly, who had come downstairs with Pippa. 'If you want to have a go at anybody — it had better be me. Look, you think you understand, but you don't. I wasn't just worried about people in Summer Bay finding out. It was you and Pippa. That's why I made them all promise to keep quiet. I was so ashamed, I didn't want you to know. I was afraid you'd think I really *had* asked for it. That's all.' She turned and went back to her room.

Pippa and Tom exchanged worried glances. 'I tried,' said Pippa.

'Maybe I'd better have a word,' said Tom. 'I suppose I was a bit rough on her, earlier . . .'

Carly was lying on her bed again when he walked in and sat down beside her. He took her hand and squeezed it. After a moment, Carly squeezed back.

Tom cleared his throat. 'Sometimes, when lousy things happen, all you feel like doing is hitting back. Then, when the person you're really angry at is out of reach, sometimes you lash out and hurt the people you care most about. I'm sorry, Carly.

'It mightn't always seem like it, but I do try to do my best for you and the other kids . . .'

'I know . . .' said Carly.

'When something like this happens, you start

thinking maybe your best isn't good enough. I feel like I've let you down.'

'*You've* let *me* down? Why?' said Carly.

'It's my job to make sure you don't come to any harm. That's what dads are for. So I suppose the one I'm really mad at is me.'

'That's silly,' said Carly, with a wan smile. 'You do your bit, Tom, believe me.'

15

Local reaction to Celia Stewart's news was mixed. Lance and Martin were solidly on Carly's side. Indeed, Martin vowed that 'the creep' would be singing soprano if Martin had his way! Lance agreed wholeheartedly.

'You've only gotta look at the way she knocked *you* back, mate,' he said owlishly to Martin.

'Yeah. Just a bit o' fun, but she wasn't having any,' agreed Martin. 'You can tell she's the pure type.'

Others were not so sure. 'I wouldn't waste my time worrying about *her*,' sneered one local who had no reason to be fond of the Fletcher family.

'What was she doin' in the car anyway?' asked others.

No, despite Tom's support and Pippa's council, it wasn't going to be easy living this down. Anyone'd think, as Carly said sourly, that she was the criminal instead of the victim.

Pippa drove the girls to school on the morning after

the storm had broken. She switched off the engine and turned squarely to face Carly.

'Look, if you want to stay at home today everybody'd understand,' she said.

'They'd understand all right!' said Carly bitterly.

'You know what I mean,' said Pippa.

'Oh well, I'll have to face them sooner or later,' said Carly. 'They'll still be here tomorrow. Thanks anyway, Pippa...' She got out of the car and hitched her bag onto her shoulder.

'Lynn and me'll take care of anyone that tries to be funny,' promised Bobby fiercely.

'Don't go getting into any fights,' warned Pippa.

'Who?' said Bobby innocently. 'Us?'

Pippa smiled reluctantly. She hoped the reaction at school wasn't going to be too bad.

As with the wider population of Summer Bay, reaction at the school was very mixed. The anti-Carly faction was led by Alison, who, by virtue of her clear diction and fondness for stating her opinions, was soon holding court in the locker area.

'My mum reckons she wouldn't be the first to get frightened and start shouting rape afterwards,' she said clearly. 'I mean, it looks a bit fishy — she didn't even report it until yesterday.'

'You're disgusting,' broke in Sandra flatly.

'Oh, yeah. Disgusting, is it? Who pulled your chain Barlow?'

128

One of Alison's satellites tugged at her sleeve and nodded meaningfully behind her. She had seen Lynn, Carly and Bobby coming along the corridor.

The clamour cut off as if a switch had been thrown, and several pairs of eyes, curious or scornful, sympathetic or sneering, turned towards Carly. Sandra raised her chin and went to meet them.

'Hey, Carly...' she said. Carly ignored her. 'Hey, Carly, I know you probably think everyone's against you, but it isn't true... I'm really sorry about what happened.'

'Thanks,' said Carly.

'I know it wasn't your fault,' went on Sandra.

'Sandra still believes in the tooth fairy, too,' sneered Alison.

Carly blushed and hurried away.

'Big mouth!' said Bobby.

Alison shrugged.

'Makes you feel really good, does it?' said Lynn furiously.

'Yeah,' said Alison.

'You're a foul creep, Miller,' said Lynn flatly.

'Wanna make something of it?' suggested Alison unpleasantly.

'Well, I'm not scared of you, if that's what you mean!'

'You leave her alone, Alison' said Sandra. 'Just because nobody would bother putting in a good word for *you*...'

The bell rang and, without haste, Alison collected her books and turned away. 'You'll keep — both of you,' she said, and strolled off.

'You don't want to worry about *her*, she isn't worth it,' said Sandra comfortingly.

While Carly was running the gauntlet of school opinion, the source of the outbreak was visiting her brother. Alf was not pleased to see her.

'I want you to know I didn't sleep a wink last night,' claimed Celia. 'I was tossing and turning ... you can imagine!'

'My heart bleeds,' said Alf sardonically.

'All those terrible things you said about me!' wailed Celia.

'About you! How about what you said about Carly?'

Celia pulled out her handkerchief and wiped her eyes.

Alf softened a bit. 'Want a cuppa?' he asked. 'Just made one.'

'Tea bags?' said Celia.

'Yeah.'

'No thank you. Look, I didn't mean the girl any harm...'

'No, you never do,' agreed Alf. 'That's the trouble.'

Celia looked thoughtful. Until now, her horror at what she had done had been at least partly assumed. Now the implications — not only to Carly and the Fletcher family, but to herself — began to penetrate her shell of self-confidence. Her forehead wrinkled in genuine concern.

'Alfred ... what am I going to do?' she asked seriously. 'Look, how about if I tell everyone I was mistaken...'

'Be good if it was that easy, wouldn't it?' said Alf. 'Just like Perry Mason. What was it they used to say? "The jury will disregard that last statement..." Only it doesn't work that way in real life, does it? The good folk of Summer Bay have already hung the poor kid.

'Look, you can't undo what you've done... but if you've got any guts you'll go and see Carly and apologise.'

'Oh, Alfred! I couldn't! What would I say?'

'You could start with "I'm sorry" and try making it sound like you mean it.'

Celia wavered. On the one hand she could see herself making the gesture... Carly accepting... problem over. On the other hand, she could see herself making the gesture, and Carly repudiating it savagely.

And she couldn't delude herself that the first view was the more realistic.

'Forgiveness is a virtue,' she said aloud.

'Yeah. Well, I wouldn't go banking too much on that, Sis,' said Alf. 'I expect young Carly'll give you curry, and who can blame her?'

Celia raised her chin nobly. 'Never mind,' she said. 'I'll do the right thing.'

'Great,' said Alf. He wondered if she would. Celia had always had grandiose ideas, but she sometimes lacked the moral courage to carry them out!

Celia left the liquor store and pushed her bike along the footpath, turning her plan over in her mind. Where

131

would be the best place to approach Carly? Perhaps she could visit her at home — or would it be better to accost her on the way home from school that afternoon?

Finally she decided to wait until school came out and then go to the Fletchers' place. It seemed altogether more fitting. And besides, after her experience with Lynn, she had had rather enough of road-side interviews.

Celia spent the rest of the day enlisting help for the church fete and then headed for the caravan park. The first people she met were Lance and Martin clutching glasses of what Celia assumed to be lemon squash. 'Afternoon, boys,' she said.

'G'day, Miss Stewart,' said Lance.

'Is that lemon squash you're drinking?' asked Celia brightly.

'Oh, umm ... you wouldn't like it. Turned out a bit funny,' faltered Martin.

'Used the wrong kind of potatoes,' added Lance.

Celia stared, but before she could sort this one out, she caught sight of Carly heading up towards the house. 'Excuse me, boys,' she said quickly. 'Carly!'

Carly glanced round and began to hurry. She'd had a lousy day at school. Fisher had actually summoned her and announced his intention of talking about her experience at tomorrow's assembly, using it as an object lesson! She glowered as she recalled his words:

'Of course I won't mention you by name... you'll be excused attendance...' She'd practically pleaded with him, but his mind was made up. And now here was Celia Stewart on the horizon!

She hurried into the house, but Celia was not to be deflected. 'Carly — please,' she said breathlessly. 'It'll only take a minute...'

Carly stopped and glared at her.

'I know you're upset,' pursued Celia, 'and I wanted a chance to apologise. I never dreamed Doris would tell anybody ... of course, that's really no excuse ... I shouldn't have told her in the first place — I just didn't think. But I do want you to know I didn't mean to hurt you. We're all so sorry about what happened — everybody is... The funny thing is, you mightn't think so now, but in the long run it's probably all for the best. These things are always better out in the open.' She swallowed. 'I am sorry, dear...'

'You finished?' demanded Carly.

'Er — yes,' said Celia. 'I know you're upset, but...'

'You don't know anything!' said Carly deliberately. 'You think you can just come in here and say sorry and everything'll be all right. Well, it won't! Everybody's talking about me because of you, and if you think I'm going to say that's all right, just so you can feel better — forget it. As far as I'm concerned, you're a rotten, dried-up old prune. All you ever do is stick your nose in where it isn't wanted and make trouble for people. No wonder no-one likes you!' She gave a coldly emphatic nod and then stalked away towards the stairs.

16

Naturally, the tirade Carly had launched at Celia Stewart didn't stay a secret. Mortified, Celia fled to Ailsa's store, and gave her version of what had happened.

'I had to talk to someone,' she wailed. 'I can't go to Alfred — he made me go and see her in the first place. Well I hope he's satisfied. You would not believe some of the things that child said to me! I just wish he'd been there! The language! Somebody ought to speak to her parents.' She mopped her eyes and look appraisingly at Ailsa.

'Me?' said Ailsa in astonishment. 'Oh no, Celia. Count me out.'

Celia's voice rose. 'She positively abused me!'

'She probably thought you deserved it,' said Ailsa roundly. 'I'm sorry, Celia, but I'm on her side in this ...'

'Oh yes ...' cried Celia. 'That's right, of course. I'm always the one in the wrong ... it wasn't easy for me going to see that girl. Nobody gives me credit for that.'

Ailsa sighed. 'Celia, I know you're not a malicious person, but you've got to face it — as far as gossip goes, you're practically an addict. Gossip can do a lot of damage. Look, you took a step in the right direction when you went to see Carly. But you've got to go all the way — kick the habit.' She laughed. 'Think of it like giving up smoking! Chew a stick of gum every time you feel the urge.'

Celia's mouth opened in indignation, then she sighed. Maybe Ailsa had a point.

That evening, Carly took a deep breath and walked into the kitchen where Pippa was cutting school lunches. Tom was sitting close by, having a cup of coffee. She sat beside him.

'What's on your mind?' asked Pippa lightly.

'You said I don't tell you things,' stumbled Carly. 'Okay, I'm telling you. Celia Stewart came here today. She wanted to apologise . . . I — um — I told her she was a dried-up old prune and nobody liked her.'

'Carly!' said Pippa.

'I'm not sorry for what I said,' continued Carly defiantly, 'and I don't want anyone apologising for me — 'cos it wouldn't be true.'

'That seems fair enough,' said Tom cautiously.

'Then there's something else,' said Carly. 'Old Flathead's going to talk about me at assembly tomorrow.'

'What!' exclaimed Pippa.

'Like hell he is!' said Tom ferociously.

'He says he's got a responsibility to the other kids,' said Carly with distaste.

Tom got up. 'I'll soon set him straight on *that* subject!' he promised.

'No, don't. Please!' said Carly. 'I've got to handle it my own way or it won't work! Look, I know what I'm doing... I just don't know if I've got the guts to do it.'

Next morning, Carly was hovering miserably in the corridor with Bobby.

'I don't believe the creepoid'd actually do it,' comforted Bobby.

' 'Course he will,' said Carly. 'Here we go...'

'You've got more guts than me,' said Bobby.

'Don't bet on it,' said Carly. She took a deep, steadying breath and strode towards the door of the Assembly Hall.

Fisher not only *would* do it, he was actually doing it right now.

'Getting into a car with a stranger is one of the stupidest things anybody can do,' he was saying. 'I know I certainly wouldn't accept a lift from someone I didn't know...'

A ripple of laughter came from the hall. Fisher made a move to quell it, and then stopped short as Carly appeared. 'What are you doing here?' he asked in amazement.

'I've got something to say myself,' said Carly.

'I don't think this is the time...' began Fisher dubiously.

'Look,' said Carly. 'It didn't happen to you. If anyone should talk about it, it's me.'

'Very well,' said Fisher, after a pause.

Carly nodded and took his place on the podium. More giggles came from the hall. Carly cleared her throat.

'You all know who he was talking about — me,' she said abruptly. 'I was dumb enough to go hitch-hiking and you all know what happened. I know some of you think I deserved it... And maybe some of you even think it's funny. Well, I don't care what you think! But... nobody deserves that, and it wasn't funny... it was the most awful thing that's ever happened to me. If anything decent can come out of it, maybe it's that what happened to me might stop it from happening to any of you. And if any of you still want to go hitch-hiking, you need your heads read. That's it.'

There were no giggles now. Carly lifted her head and stared defiantly round the hall, but somehow the faces were blurring and wavering before her gaze.

Fisher moved in hastily. 'Thank you, Miss Morris,' he said. His dry voice broke the spell and Carly left the hall.

After school, Sandra went to Ailsa's store to buy some fuse wire. She hung over the counter chattering happily about Carly's stand at assembly that morning.

'She was just incredible,' she reported with enthusiasm. 'She had the whole school onside by the end.'

138

'Good for her!' said Ailsa. She had once had to run the gauntlet of Summer Bay gossip herself, and she was genuinely delighted to hear of Carly's success.

'Steven and I wanted to get them clapping,' confided Sandra, 'but Fisher wouldn't've approved. Betcha.'

Ailsa laughed. 'Not the done thing at assembly, what?' she said in a pompous imitation of Fisher's manner.

'Right on,' said Sandra.

'There you are, love,' said Ailsa, handing over Sandra's change. 'Having some trouble with the fuses at home?'

'No, it's for my science project. Radio transmitter. See ya!'

Ailsa grinned and nodded as Sandra hurried out. Her smile wavered as someone emerged from behind the tinned peas. It was Celia Stewart.

'I couldn't help overhearing, Ailsa dear!' said Celia breathlessly.

'Really? From all the way over there?'

'Sound carries,' said Celia.

'Does if your ears flap enough,' said Ailsa.

'Well! There's no need to be like that!' said Celia. 'Look, Ailsa, I've no reason to like young Carly, after her insolence, but I have to admit it: it sounds like she was really brave.'

'I thought you wanted to kick the gossip habit?' muttered Ailsa.

'I'm not gossiping, I'm only...'

'Gossiping,' supplied Ailsa.

'... discussing a mutual acquaintance, I *was* going to say,' corrected Celia. 'I mean to say, what are you supposed to think when a girl...'

'I thought you weren't going to gossip?' said Ailsa. Solemnly, she took down a packet of chewing gum. 'I meant it as a joke yesterday,' she said, 'but desperate times call for desperate measures. Whenever that tongue of yours starts wagging, chew on this instead of other people's reputations.'

'Do you really...'

'That's my advice,' added Ailsa in a louder tone. 'Take it or leave it.'

Celia hesitated, turning her gaze from the gum to Ailsa's implacable face. She took the gum.

17

After leaving Ailsa, Celia went round to the Fletcher place. She parked her bike near the door and knocked.

'Come in!' yelled Tom, from where he was replacing a washer at the kitchen tap. 'Not locked!'

Celia popped her head through the door. 'Hard at it, I see!' she chirped as she advanced.

'G'day, Celia,' said Tom resignedly. 'Leaky tap. Never stops dribbling. Runs on and on just like... well, it never stops.'

Celia nodded sympathetically. 'They don't make things the way they used to,' she said.

'Well, what can I do for you?' asked Tom.

Celia came right out with it. 'Is Carly here?'

'Sorry,' said Tom. Few things about Celia Stewart could surprise him, but it did occur to him to wonder that even Celia had a thick enough skin to come back for another dose.

'I wanted to congratulate her on her courage this morning,' said Celia.

'Around town, is it?'

141

'And deserves to be,' said Celia emphatically. 'She's a fine young girl. Standing up like that to drive such an important message home. Girls who hitch-hike . . . it's insanity.'

'Couldn't agree more,' said Tom. 'Though,' he added slyly, 'from what I hear of your row, I'm surprised you're bothering.'

'Her sentiments were . . . shall we say . . . forcefully expressed . . . unnecessarily hurtful, but we must remember that the girl had been through a traumatic experience. Forgiveness is a virtue. Well, if she's not here, I can't stop. Just let her know I called.'

She turned away and Tom bent back to his work. He looked up wearily as Celia suddenly remembered something. 'Oh — by the way,' she said, 'I suppose you've already heard . . .' She broke off suddenly, grabbed a piece of gum and put it into her mouth.

'You okay there?' asked Tom.

'It's gossip,' said Celia indistinctly.

'What is?'

'What I was about to say. So I won't say it. Not after the distress I caused Carly.'

'Good idea,' applauded Tom. 'But why the gum?'

'Well, you see, it was Ailsa's idea, really. She suggested that every time I . . . oh, never mind. The thing is, I'm determined to keep out of other people's business. Goodbye.'

And she left, cycling down the road and being very careful not to catch anyone's eye. She didn't even notice the bus from the city . . . which caused her to miss out on a very choice bit of gossip indeed.

After he'd finished in the kitchen, Tom busied himself with some jobs out in the caravan park. Sally hung around, watching.

'Hey look,' she interrupted. 'It's Floss! And she's got a boy with her!'

'Hi! Didn't know you were coming home,' commented Tom, as Floss and her companion approached.

'Nope, it was a spur-of-the-moment thing,' said Floss happily. 'Ben and me felt like a break, so we got the bus. Hi, Sal! This is Ben, the boy I'm looking after. Ben, this is Sally. Look, how about you two kids get to know one another while I go and have a word with Nev?' She turned away from Ben and winked at Tom. 'He won't half be surprised to see us,' she commented.

'And *that* must be the understatement of the year,' muttered Tom to himself. He raised his voice. 'Just a minute, Floss...' He took her aside and continued more quietly: 'I gather Ben's your grandson?'

'That's right,' said Floss proudly.

'Nev said he wouldn't have him here.'

'That's right,' repeated Floss.

'He sounded pretty determined,' warned Tom.

Floss patted his shoulder. 'So am I, lovey, so am I!'

It was a bright, fine afternoon, with a bracing breeze blowing in from the bay. Seagulls swooped and quarrelled on the beach, and pelicans fished near the jetty.

The seagulls weren't the only ones quarrelling this afternoon. The McPhees were at it again.

Tom had been quite right. Neville was not pleased.

'I don't ask much of you, Floss,' he complained. 'So you could at least respect the few things a man *does* ask!'

'I want you to get to know each other,' said Floss stubbornly.

'Why bother?' said Neville.

'Because he's your grandson, you stubborn old coot!' howled Floss.

'You know what'll happen when Scotty comes back,' warned Neville.

'Ben'll love us by then,' said Floss contentedly. 'Don't you see? If Scotty gets back and Ben loves us, he won't have the heart to keep us apart!'

'Don't count on it,' grunted Neville.

The argument ran back and forth for some time, but finally Neville sighed and capitulated. 'Okay, okay, he can stay. But there'll be trouble, so don't say I didn't warn you.'

Floss hugged him. 'I love you, you cantankerous galoot,' she said. 'I'll go and bring him in.'

'No, don't do that,' said Neville hastily. He walked to the door of the van and looked out to where Ben was playing out in the park. 'So that's him, eh?' he said.

'Yeah,' said Floss, hugging his arm. 'Isn't he a little cracker?'

'Humph,' said Neville.

Ben enjoyed his afternoon. He played ball with Sally's dog and squabbled with Sally, running around the

144

park and inspecting the beach. Only at night did the novelty begin to pall.

It was dark and creepy, and then Neville began to snore. Ben stood it for as long as he could, and then went across the van to shake Neville by the shoulder.

'Hey!' he said indignantly.

'What? What's up?' grunted Neville.

'What . . .?' echoed Floss.

'He's snoring,' said Ben bluntly. 'I can't sleep. He's making too much noise.'

'You cheeky little devil!' exclaimed Neville.

'Now calm down,' said Floss. 'I know he can be noisy, love, but he's stopped now. You just go back to bed.'

'What if he starts again?' said Ben suspiciously.

'You can lie there and put up with it!' said Neville furiously. Ben went back to bed and Neville muttered: 'Damn kid. As cheeky as his dad was at that age.'

'Just like his dad, eh?' whispered Floss sadly. 'Aren't you just a little bit glad he's come, though?'

Neville didn't answer, but Floss was comforted. She knew that, whatever happened, she wouldn't regret this brief time she had been given to spend with her grandson.

It didn't matter how long it lasted, or what happened afterwards, she'd had this gift from fate, and she knew that nothing could ever take it away from her.

Epilogue

The four elder Fletcher kids were drying up when Bobby came in.

'Hey — look what I got!' she hissed, and held up a neatly folded fifty-dollar note.

'Hey! Been robbing the bank?' asked Steven.

Bobby looked virtuous. 'Nah. I came by it honest as the day — almost,' she said. Tantalisingly, she tucked the note in her pocket and took up a towel.

'Well, go on,' urged Lynn after a moment.

'Go on what?' said Bobby.

'Tell us how you got the money,' said Steven. 'We wanna know, don't we, Carls?'

Carly shrugged, but she looked interested.

'Go on,' said Frank.

Bobby sighed happily. 'It was that bloody still of Lance's,' she said.

'*What* was?' demanded Lynn.

'The start,' said Bobby. 'See, I was out the other day an' I found this cat wanderin' round the vans. I took it to Lance's van.'

'Why?' asked Lynn.

'Dunno,' said Bobby. 'I was goin' out, an' I didn't want it to get mixed up with any nutters, did I? Thought I'd see about it when I got back. Anyhow, I sort of forgot — till the next mornin', when I ran into Fisher. I nearly backed off — I mean *Fisher*?'

'Fisher's not so bad,' said Carly.

Bobby glowered. 'Before *breakfast*?' she said. 'Anyhow, he called out an' said had I seen a cat. Nearly said I had, then he said how he'd lost this valuable brown cat — Papageno, he called it — and he was about to offer fifty dollars reward. *Well*, I didn't let on I'd seen his precious Pappadums just then: thought I'd better go an' make sure he was still there, first. Well — you know Lance an' Martin . . .

'Fisher went off an' I went an' stirred 'em up. Or tried to. Well! I knocked like fury, an' nothin' happened.'

'The cat had clawed them to death?' said Steven hopefully.

'Nah, but they'd nearly done for the cat! There's Lance an' Mart out flat — been groggin' on, I reckon, only *they* called it "testin' the product"! An' poor ol' Papageno!'

'What?' said Lynn anxiously.

'Drunk as a skunk,' said Bobby solemnly. 'There he was, lappin' away at a puddle of the filthy stuff on the floor. "Oh, no!" I said. I mean, his eyes were sort of spacy and his tail all woggly. He was purrin' an' hiccuppin' at the same time.'

'You're pulling our legs,' said Steven suspiciously.

148

'Cross me heart — well, not about the hiccups.' said Bobby. ' "Don't drink that. It'll kill ya!" I told him. But he was pickled all right.'

'What'd you do?' asked Lynn.

'I chucked a glass of water at Lance an' Martin an' told 'em to sober up the cat,' said Bobby. 'An' you know what the two galahs did? Tried to make the poor bleedin' animal drink black coffee! "Do you know who this cat belongs to?" I said. They nearly passed out when I told 'em.

'Anyhow, then Lance gets another great idea. Whaddya reckon?'

The others looked blank.

'Chalk,' said Bobby.

'Chalk? To cure a hangover?' said Frank. 'That's a new one.'

'Not to cure a hangover,' said Bobby. 'Lance wanted to see if the poor bloody cat could still walk a straight line!

' "Get real, Lance!" I told him. "Cats don't walk lines," but you know old Lance once he gets an idea in his scone. He had Martin put Papageno down on the line.'

'Did he walk it?' asked Steven curiously.

Bobby gave him a pitying look. 'Whaddya reckon, brain? Of course he didn't walk it. What he did was take off an' go to roost up on the bunk. Fair climbin' the walls, he was. Then o' course, Lance makes a dive for him. Right across the table. Splat!'

'Did he break anything?' asked Lynn anxiously.

'Yeah, two cups of coffee. Oh, you mean *Lance*. Nah, he's okay: got a head like a cannonball anyhow. He knocked Martin over, too, and they got all tangled up,' Bobby shook her head.

'What happened next?' asked Lynn breathlessly.

'Well, there they were, strewn all over the bloody van like week-old stiffs — 'cept they were moanin' an' groanin',' said Bobby. 'An' the cat was perched up on top o' Lance's bunk, squallin'.'

'Yes? And?' prompted Frank, as Bobby paused to laugh. 'Oh, and keep your voice down, Bob. Pippa'll be down soon. She's just getting Sal to bed.'

Steven and Lynn had already discarded their tea towels, so Bobby beckoned the others in closer. '*So*,' she said, 'I goes along and gets old Fisher, don't I? Tell him I've found his fancy cat and all? So Lance an' Martin got the still all shut down an' gave the van a good old airin' out — smelt like a brewery in there...'

'Why didn't you just go and tell Mr Fisher?' asked Lynn.

Bobby looked sly. 'There was the matter o' the reward,' she said.

Frank looked interested. 'Yeah? The fifty bucks?'

'That's it,' said Bobby. '*Well*, I fetched Fisher along and gave 'im back his Papageno (in front of witnesses), and he gave me the fifty bucks, and what d'you know? Lance an' Martin reckoned they oughta get a cut!'

'What for?' asked Steven. 'Keeping him in the van?'

Bobby shook her head. 'Nah, because they reckoned they'd sobered 'im up. I mean to say — *who got him drunk in the first place*?'

She began to laugh, and the others joined in. First Steven, then Frank and Lynn, and finally Carly. They laughed so much and so loudly that Pippa came in.

'What's the joke?' she asked mildly.

They looked at one another.

'I vote we tell her!' said Carly suddenly.

'No!' yelled Bobby, Frank, Lynn and Steven.

'Yes!' said Carly. 'I reckon she can keep her mouth shut! Listen, Pippa, you know those potato peelings you gave Sal to give to Lance...?'